Clara E. C. Waters

Saints in Art

Clara E. C. Waters

Saints in Art

ISBN/EAN: 9783337335922

Printed in Europe, USA, Canada, Australia, Japan

Cover: Foto ©Andreas Hilbeck / pixelio.de

More available books at **www.hansebooks.com**

SAINTS IN ART

BY
CLARA ERSKINE CLEMENT

AUTHOR OF
"A HANDBOOK OF LEGENDARY ART,"
"PAINTERS, SCULPTORS, ARCHITECTS, AND ENGRAVERS,"
"ARTISTS OF THE NINETEENTH CENTURY,"
ETC.

Illustrated

LONDON
DAVID NUTT
1899

.

Colonial Press:
Electrotyped and Printed by C. H. Simonds & Co.
Boston. U. S. A.

CONTENTS.

———◆———

ILLUSTRATIONS.

SAINTS IN ART.

CHAPTER I.

CONCERNING THE REPRESENTATIONS OF SAINTS IN ART.

IN the study of Art, the pictures and statues of saints are so numerous and so important, that if one adds to the contemplation and enjoyment of their effigies the study of their lives, historical and legendary, he acquires a sense of acquaintance with a great number of holy and intrepid men and women.

An interest is also added to one's thought and study, that greatly contributes to the comprehension of the age in which religious art was the chief art, and of the men who lived and worked in that age; while the increased enjoyment of the legacies of that epoch abundantly repays the student for any effort he has made.

The history of the world, from the time of the Exodus to the present day, constantly emphasises the truth that freedom, civil or religious, is only secured at a costly price. A large proportion of those whom we call saints — the most exalted title that is conferred on human beings — sacrificed their lives rather than renounce Christianity, while history warrants us in estimating a great number of these as heroes and heroines of superhuman courage and loyalty to their convictions, both as Christians and patriots.

Supplementing history, tradition and legendary chronicles have contributed generously to their honour and glory, all of which has been exalted and spiritualised by poets and artists, until the phrase, stories of the saints, calls up to the imagination a world of heroism, romance, religious enthusiasm, profound faith, and living spirituality, in which every one may find a personality which appeals to his own nature, and excites both his sympathy with the saint, and a spirit of emulation of the saintly virtues.

It is impossible to intelligently judge the religion and thought of a people, without a knowledge of the atmosphere in which they existed, and though but a few centuries separate us from the Middle Ages, it is only by persistent investigation that we can so understand the life of that period as to — even in an imperfect degree — bring ourselves into harmony with the spirit and purpose of the great masters, to whom we owe the earliest representations of saints, and other religious pictures.

In regard to many saints, it is true that the incidents in their lives, which seized upon the imagination of the artists, and were pictured by them, rested on legendary, rather than historical, authority. But even the most improbable legends had some slight basis of truth.

We must remember that the saints who had died for their faith in Christ were brought close to the people through oral tradition and legendary chronicles at a period when Christians — with the exception of the very learned — had not the Gospel to study, and could scarcely realise a nearness to Him, concerning whose nature they were hopelessly puzzled by the wrangling of the schoolmen.

In truth, the *people* of the Middle Ages were separated from Christ by an impassable barrier of theological speculation, in which they had no share, while to the saints and martyrs they could draw near, and — as Milman has pointed out — their reverence became adoration, and the line drawn by theology between the honour due to God and Christ, and that due to saints and martyrs, was lost sight of in the sympathy of all classes for human beings who, with no claim to divinity, yet displayed virtues which could only be characterised as divine.

Modern, or Western, art, may be said to have had its birth about the seventh century A. D., and to have contended through three hundred years with a feeble infancy, when, slightly waxing in strength, it gradually attained to the virility of the fifteenth and sixteenth centuries.

During the earliest periods of its life, the *people* were generously fed with the stories of the adventures and the wonderful deeds of heroes. These stories were read and recited in public, for the benefit of those who wished to hear. When the recital was purely historical the truth was simply miraculous to the unlearned, and the legendary story, when added, was no more wonderful to them than the truth had been, and was, therefore, as readily accepted and as sincerely believed.

We must also remember that in the Middle Ages might was right, and every sort of oppression was suffered by the weaker classes, from the stronger, whose only profession was that of war; and this vocation, followed through successive generations, so brutalised these warriors that kindness and mercy, and even common humanity, were almost extinct, while gentle and refining influences in the ordinary relations of life were quite unknown. It was a period in the history of the world when repose and safety were non-existent outside the cloister, whither both men and women fled to escape persecution, and to preserve their personal purity.

With these conditions in mind we can understand that the stories of the saints must have given courage and comfort to the weary and downtrodden people who were as ignorant as they were heavy-laden,—stories which inspired a belief in the existence of love and tenderness and courage in both men and women ; stories which proved that there were those who for conscience' sake protested against the evil surrounding them, and even died, rather than sin in word or deed; stories which assured them of a heaven, of the existence of angels, and of powers that could even overcome Satan himself, and guide the spirit of the timid, fainting Christian to the presence of a tender, omnipotent Saviour.

During these centuries the most extravagant legends of the saints, which were the daily food of the people, gained such an influence and were believed so absolutely that, when the Church endeavoured by edicts and councils to put aside these exaggerations, she found herself powerless, and was forced to patiently endeavour to modify rather than abolish these extravagances.

It was largely through the influence of Art that the Church instructed the ignorant; she appealed to their better nature through painting, sculpture, and music. It was impossible to exclude at once such subjects as were objectionable to the intelligent class of that age, and greater wisdom was shown by using a more moderate policy, rather than by instituting a violent opposition to errors which were the logical outcome of such darkness as had so long prevailed. //

Churches afforded the opportunity for religious scene painting, and, repulsive as many of these decorations are to the present spirit of the Christian world, we must respect them for having served their purpose, in an age when education, civilisation, and refinement were too feeble to neutralise the forces that opposed them. In many of these works such sincerity is manifested, and so enduring a spirit of devotion, that they deeply interest us, although we cannot accept them in the childlike spirit of the reverential Christians of the age in which they were created.

Thousands of travellers visit these shrines, a large proportion of whom comprehend but little of their meaning, and thus lose the profit which should come from an acquaintance with the monuments of any religious faith which has served as a stimulant to spirituality in the dimly lighted periods of the world's history.

The symbolism of the saints is little understood by many who visit churches and picture-galleries. One soon learns that the man who bristles with arrows is St. Sebastian, and, without a knowledge of the reason for this, his picture is supremely absurd, while the frequency with which he presents himself becomes a huge joke. The man of the gridiron is speedily recognised as St. Lawrence, and several of the more pronounced symbols are known *as symbols*, with no knowledge of what they symbolise. Of the less prominent emblems still less is apprehended, and the effect which these works of art should produce is lost. While we may enjoy the picture as a picture, or the sculpture as a product of art, the subtile meaning, the impalpable element which should stir our hearts, floats over our heads, and leaves us essentially ignorant of what we have seen; a means of profit and pleasure has been offered one, and he has not taken his share of it because he is so ill prepared for its enjoyment.

In the study of pictures of the saints, as in the study of all religious art, it is of the first importance to keep the distinction between devotional and historical representations clearly in mind. Devotional pictures present to us beings worthy of veneration simply as sacred personages; these may be in numbers, or as single figures, but must be *void of action*.

When such personages are represented as performing miracles, doing good works, suffering martyrdom, or taking their part in any Scriptural or other sacred story, we have a distinctly historical subject.

The representation of the Virgin Mary with the Infant Jesus, either alone or surrounded by angels and saints, is the de-

votional subject which is dearest to the
world.   The wonderful representations of
Paradise, the Last Judgment, the Adoration of the Lamb, and kindred subjects,
in which the Almighty and Christ in
Glory are surrounded by all the orders
of sacred beings, from God and his Son
to the humble confessors of the Christian
faith, are the grandest and most impressive of devotional pictures, as one realises
in beholding the Paradise of Fra Angelico, in the Academy of Florence, the
Last Judgment of Orcagna, in the Campo
Santo of Pisa, or the Adoration of the
Lamb by Van Eyck, in the Church of
St. Bavon at Ghent.

The representation of the Joys and Sorrows of the Virgin by Hans Memling, in
the Munich Gallery, is a good example
of the so-called historical picture.   There
are many figures, and all are in action.
The Virgin adores the new-born child;

VAN DER GOES. — ST. ANTHONY AND ST. MATTHEW.
(VOTIVE PICTURE OF TOMMASO PORTINARI)

the Wise Men worship Him, and present
their gifts; Jesus heals the Sick; the
Procession of the Cross ascends to Cal-
vary; in short, the Seven Sorrows and
the Seven Joys of the Virgin are all depicted as actually occurring before our
eyes.

There are numerous votive pictures,
that is, pictures painted in fulfilment of
a vow, in gratitude for some especial blessing, or to avert some threatening danger.
In such works, the donor, and sometimes his entire family, are introduced in
the picture, as in the celebrated Meier
Madonna by Holbein, in the Dresden ✕
Gallery.

In the earlier votive pictures, the humility of the donors was often expressed
by the diminutive size in which they were
painted; later they appeared in their natural proportions. In a picture in which
a bishop kneels while the other figures

stand, he is the donor. Nearly all votive
pictures are devotional, as they usually
represent the donors as paying their
homage to the Madonna or to patron
saints.

There are pictures, however, that at
the first glance appear to be devotional,
that are in reality historical. For example, in the Marriage of St. Catherine,
although the saint kneels in an attitude
of profound devotion, there is the action
of giving and receiving the ring, which
at once makes the picture historical.

Both historical and devotional pictures
may be either Scriptural or legendary.
The first will rarely require explanation
to one acquainted with the Bible. In
legendary pictures of the saints, historical
subjects usually represent miracles or
martyrdoms; the latter are always painful,
and frequently revolting; the former are
essentially reproductions of such miracles

as are described in the Scriptures. Thus the saints are presented as living counterparts of Christ and his disciples.

Naturally, a large proportion of purely devotional pictures portray a single saint as one to whom veneration is due, but there is also a class of very interesting pictures which represent a group of saints in repose, as, for example, in a beautiful work by Andrea del Sarto, in the Academy in Florence, in which the two elements, the devotional and historical, are strikingly combined. On the left are SS. Michael and John Gualberto in repose, — devotional; on the right are SS. John the Baptist and Bernard, the former with his right hand raised earnestly talking to St. Bernard, who listens attentively, — historical.

The Italians have a special name for a group of sacred persons in repose, and call it a *sacra conversazione;* this last word does

not essentially mean a conversation in the
sense of speech, but rather a communion;
thus, a communion of holy beings is the
best definition of the above phrase, as here
employed with singular fitness. Such
pictures are often very beautiful, and
appeal to one more than do the representations of miracles and other extraordi-
nary acts. Many enthroned Madonnas,
surrounded by saints, belong to this class,
as does one of the best pictures by Perugino, in the Bologna Gallery, in which the
Virgin enthroned holds the child, standing, on her knee. They are surrounded
by seraphim with wings of brilliant colour.
Below are SS. Michael, Catherine, Apollonia and John the Baptist. It is interesting to note that here St. John is an old
man, the saint who had beheld the vision
of the Revelation, and is in strong contrast to the eternal youth of St. Michael.

Purely legendary historical subjects, in

pictures of the saints, are those in which they walk upon the water, are fed miraculously, are delivered from suffering by angels, and so on, while their exercise of miraculous-power is most frequently depicted in the healing of the sick, casting out evil spirits, and restoring the dead to life.

Other legendary subjects represent a mingling of Scripture and history, as in pictures of SS. Paul and Peter. In these the Bible story and the traditions of the Church are so combined that care must be taken in order to distinguish history from legend. Again they illustrate purely fabulous traditions, while in others religious truths are figuratively set forth, in the same sense that the "Pilgrim's Progress" is an allegorical legend.

Anachronisms are especially apparent in pictures of saints, but if one will remember that such representations were

intended to express the devotional spirit
rather than to represent physical facts, it
will not seem so out of reason that St.
Jerome should present his translation of
the Scriptures to the Infant Jesus, while
an angel turns the leaves; nor that poets
and philosophers who died before Christ
was born on earth should present to him
scrolls inscribed with sentences from their
writings which are regarded as prophecies
of his coming.

Saints that apparently have no relation
to each other may be portrayed in company because the picture was painted for
a locality in which, at varying periods,
these saints have been venerated as patrons of the region. For example, St.
Theodore and St. Mark may be coupled
for no other reason than that one preceded
the other as patron saint of Venice; as
St. Mark, St. George, and St. Catherine
would be curiously bizarre in each other's

society did they not divide the honours as contemporary patrons of the Queen of the Adriatic.

St. Roch and St. Sebastian are associated because the latter was the patron against the plague, and the former cared for those who suffered from it. SS. Stephen and Lawrence appear as companions in works of art, not because they were such when living, but because they were entombed together.

These examples show what research will prove to be true, that such representations as are surprising and incongruous to us rested on a sufficiently reasonable basis in the mind of the artist; one should respectfully learn the reasons for such apparent inconsistencies before he ridicules or despises them.

Besides the patron saints of certain localities, there are those which may be termed the patrons of Christendom, and may legitimately appear in pictures of all countries. These are SS. George, Sebastian, Christopher, Cosmo, Damian, Roch, Nicholas, Catherine, Barbara, Margaret, and Ursula.

Again, saints who were not associated when living were united as protecting patrons of organisations that laboured for the poor and the fallen, ransomed slaves and redeemed prisoners; one such society relied on SS. Peter, Leonard, Martha, and Mary Magdalene, — St. Peter because he had been a prisoner; St. Leonard, because he laboured for the good of slaves and captives in his life; St. Martha on account of her charity and benevolence; and St. Mary Magdalene, because she is the patroness of frail and penitent women.

Thus it is that what first appears to be fantastic and unsuitable, when understood and appreciated, adds value and a deeper meaning to such religious art as we are

considering. It aids us in discerning its
sentiment and intention, and proves that
what, at a cursory glance, seems the result of an ignorance of the fitness of
things, is, in truth, the expression of
earnest, devotional thought, of spiritual
and poetic intelligence, and a desire to
imbue that which will give pleasure to the
eye with spiritual and uplifting significance.

An explanation of the symbolism connected with saints in Art will be found in
the appendix.

CHAPTER II.

THE EVANGELISTS.

THE Evangelists were very frequently represented in ancient art by symbols rather than in human form. Their earliest symbols, the four scrolls or books, emblematic of the Gospels, or the four rivers of Salvation flowing from Paradise, are seen in the Catacombs and on the walls of the oldest existing churches, or on relics hoary with age, as the earliest Christian sarcophagi and tombs.

In the fifth century the "Four Beasts," which had already been used as emblems of the Four Archangels and the Four Great Prophets, were adopted as symbols

34

of the Evangelists; and two centuries
later these curious creatures were universally employed as symbolic of these four
saints. At first they were simply emblems of the Evangelists, but after St.
Jerome wrote of the Vision of Ezekiel,
each of these beasts was assigned to a
particular saint. To St. Matthew was
given the Cherub or winged human face;
to St. Mark the Lion; to St. Luke the
Ox, and to St. John the Eagle.

The reasons for this assignment are
usually explained by saying that the more
human symbol is appropriate to the Evangelist who traces the human ancestry of
Christ; the Lion to him whose gospel
of Jesus Christ begins with "the voice of
one crying in the wilderness;" the Ox to
him who writes especially of the priesthood and of sacrifice, of which the ox is
symbolical; and the Eagle to him whose
inspiration soared to the loftiest heights,

and enabled him to reach the paramount
human perception of the dual nature of
Jesus Christ.

These symbols and that called the Tet-
ramorph — a mysterious winged figure
uniting the four symbols — are frequently
seen in works of art. There are also
several variations of them, as, for example,
figures of men with the heads of the
Beasts, or the Beasts holding books or
scrolls, all of which are representations of
the Evangelists.

Such symbolic pictures were perfectly
intelligible to the early Christians, and
were sacred in their eyes. As late as the
sixteenth century the Evangelists were
expressed by these emblems in both pictures and statues, an example still existing in the symbolic bronzes in the choir
of the Church of St. Antonio, at Padua,
which are very unusual and interesting.

These symbols were not, however, uni-

versally used to personate the Evangelists,
even in the early centuries, since in the
mosaics and manuscripts of the sixth century the Evangelists are depicted as venerable men, with their symbols near them.

Neither Michael Angelo, Raphael, nor
Leonardo da Vinci represented the Four
Evangelists in their special office. Raphael introduced St. John in the splendid
group of Apostles, Prophets, and Saints
in La Disputa, where he is placed between Adam and King David; and in his
famous picture of the Vision of Ezekiel,
in the Pitti Gallery in Florence, the Saviour is borne aloft by the Four Beasts;
in the St. Cecilia, too, in the Bologna
Gallery, he also represented the Beloved
Disciple, but the writers of the Gospels, as
a group, he did not paint.

Likewise Leonardo, in his well-known
Last Supper, in Santa Maria delle Grazie,
Milan, represented them as disciples, but

not as Evangelists; and in the same manner they appear as apostles, in the frescoes of Michael Angelo, in the Sistine Chapel.

From the thirteenth to the seventeenth centuries the figures of the Evangelists appeared in all elaborate schemes of theological decoration. Their usual position was under the domes of churches or chapels, where they were placed after the angels and prophets who surrounded the central figure of the Saviour. Domes thus decorated by Cimabue in Assisi, by Giotto in Ravenna, by Fra Angelico in the Vatican, by Perugino in Perugia, and by Correggio in Parma, are noteworthy examples of these frescoes, while that by Domenichino, in St. Andrea della Valle in Rome, is esteemed as his masterpiece; here angels are represented as sporting around the lion, and toying with his mane; others play with the palette and pencils of St. Luke, and are extremely attractive as pictures, though not ideal as angels.

Allegorical figures of women are grouped about the Evangelists, superb in pose and bearing; one, nude above the waist, raises her arms to heaven; another, with a helmet, is the personification of haughty pride. There is an element of paganism in this famous work; powerful and picturesque, one does not forget it, although it scarcely accords with the Christian conception of the Evangelists. The figure of St. John, however, is of quite a different type from the others; it is beautiful in expression and in colour.

These frescoes were severely criticised during Domenichino's life, and it is related that he visited them some time after their completion, and, after studying them, exclaimed, " It does not appear so bad to me," and many who now see them, two

and a half centuries after his death, agree
with his estimate of them.

In the later pictures of the Evangelists,
when each one is simply a man — with
his name written near him — holding a
book, his own exegesis of the Christian
doctrine, they lose something of the ideal
element imparted to them by the symbols
which served to dignify them by an association with the prophecies of the Old
Testament, as well as to distinguish them
from the other apostles.

For example, *St. Matthew* ranks as the
seventh or eighth among the apostles,
while as an Evangelist he is first, having
written his Gospel earlier than the others.
He was known as Levi before his calling
by Jesus, and was a tax-gatherer. The
Scripture account of him is slight; it
simply relates that the Master called him
as he sat at the receipt of customs; that
he at once obeyed the call, and later made

JACOPO CHIMENTI. — THE CALLING OF ST. MATTHEW.

a feast at his house, to which Jesus and his disciples went, as well as many pub-licans and sinners; for this cause the Pharisees questioned the authority of the Master, to which Christ replied, " I am not come to call the righteous, but sinners to repentance."

The legends connected with St. Mat-thew are scanty, and even the manner of his death is unknown. When represented as an apostle, his symbol is a purse or money-bag, referring to his occupation as a tax-gatherer.

The principal event in his life which has appealed to artists is his calling, and this has been frequently represented. In the Academy of Florence is a picture of this scene by Jacopo Chimenti, called Em-poli. This artist was an imitator of Andrea del Sarto. In the foreground of the picture are Christ and Matthew; the former, in full, graceful drapery, with a luminous halo, turns his gentle face towards Matthew, and extends his right hand, as if saying, " Follow me." Matthew, with his hands clasped on his breast, and his head inclined toward Jesus, has an expression of reverential love, and, apparently, waits but for the command. In the background are six men, two of whom — an old and a young man — watch the Saviour and his new disciple with intense interest, from a desk raised above the heads of the others. The expression on all the faces is excellent; the grouping and the use of light and shade remind one of the excellent master whom Chimenti aspired to imitate.

The same subject, by Pordenone, is in the Dresden Gallery, and the Mendicante of Bologna commissioned Ludovico Caracci to represent this scene, which he did in a large and effective picture.

A number of scenes from the life of

St. Matthew may be seen in churches and galleries. In the museum at Brussels, an excellent picture by F. Pourbus, the younger, is called St. Matthew and an Angel, and the same subject by Caravaggio is in the Berlin Museum; it is supposed to represent the dictation of St. Matthew's Gospel by the heavenly messenger.

In the Museum of Madrid is the Calling of St. Matthew by Juan de Pareja, the colour-grinder of Velasquez, who became an artist secretly. The St. Matthew is his most important work.

But a picture of world-wide fame connected with the life of St. Matthew, is that by Veronese, in the Academy of Venice, — where it fills one wall of the room in which it hangs, — representing the Supper at the House of Levi. It is one of a number of magnificent banquet scenes by this great artist, and while in-

tended to emphasise the luxury which
Levi left to become Matthew, it more
fitly depicts the splendour of Venice at
the height of her glory.

One wonders that such a representation
should have been considered suitable to
the decoration of a convent, but it was
painted for that of St. John and St. Paul
at Venice. Although claiming to repro-
duce a Scriptural scene, it is a most worldly
feast, such as Veronese loved to paint.
His tables in these banquet pictures are
loaded with vases and other objects in
crystal and in precious metals, and surrounded by sensuous men and women in
all the gorgeousness of silks, satins, and
velvets of richest dyes, ornamented with
rare laces, exquisite embroideries and
priceless jewels. The architecture of his
banquet-halls is grand, with their marble
porticoes through which comes such a
light as imparts a poetic vitality to the
whole scene.

Well did Taine say that if Titian is sovereign of the Venetian school of painting, Veronese is its regent; "what he loves is expanded beauty, the flower in full bloom, but intact, just when its rosy petals unfold themselves while none of them are, as yet, withered."

Imposing as this Feast of Levi is, it is not one of the best of this master's works.

Although *St. Mark* is the second Evangelist, he was not an apostle, nor even a Christian until after the Death and Ascension of Our Lord, when he was converted by St. Peter, whom he attended to Rome. In that city St. Mark's Gospel was written for the use of the converts; some authorities teach that this was dictated by St. Peter.

St. Mark founded the church at Alexandria, and by his miracles in that city so infuriated the people, who believed him

to be a magician, that they bound him
and dragged him to death. His Christian
followers placed his remains in a tomb
which was greatly venerated. Here his
body rested from A. D. 68 until about
815, when his relics were stolen by some
Venetian merchants and carried to their
city, where he has since been honoured
as its patron saint. The magnificent Basilica of St. Mark was built above his
second tomb, and the legends connected
with him have been fully illustrated, especially by Venetian artists.

In the devotional pictures of St. Mark
the winged lion is seen, almost without
exception; it is by the wings that the lion
of St. Mark is distinguished from that of
St. Jerome, and few examples are known
in which the wings are omitted from the
symbol of the Evangelist. His dress is
usually that of a Greek bishop. The
mosaic above the entrance to his Basilica,

designed by Titian, and executed by Zuccati, is a grand example of these devotional subjects. It presents the saint in pontifical robes, with no mitre, a gray beard and hair of the same colour; one hand is raised in benediction, and the Gospel is held in the other.

Perhaps the most famous devotional picture of St. Mark is that by Fra Bartolommeo. It was painted for his own convent of San Marco, in Florence, and is now in the Pitti Gallery. It is a colossal work, and is often compared with the Prophets in the Sistine Chapel by Michael Angelo; here the Evangelist is represented in the prime of life; he holds the Gospel and a pen, the lion being omitted; he is grave and grand rather than spirited. I fail to be impressed by this work as many good judges of it are, probably because I am not satisfied with a picture of a man in a niche, on a flat surface, as in this case. In sculpture the effect of this arrangement is far different, but in a picture it is not agreeable to me. However, I am here in a very small minority, as this St. Mark is one of the noted pictures in a gallery so rich in great works as is the Pitti. For this picture Ferdinand II., almost two centuries ago, paid a sum equal to nearly fifteen thousand dollars in our money.

The legendary pictures of St. Mark are very numerous, and the votive pictures, in which he is the principal personage, while the others are portraits of the donor with his family or friends, are most interesting. A beautiful example of these by Tintoretto is in the Berlin Gallery. St. Mark is enthroned with his Gospel open on his knees, while three of the Procuratori di San Marco, those who had the care of the Basilica and its treasury, in their rich crimson robes, kneel before him,

and reverently listen to his instructions.
A number of votive pictures represent St.
Mark as presenting a Doge, or some other
prominent Venetian, to the Madonna.

Another class of votive pictures illustrates the legend that St. Mark was simply
the amanuensis of St. Peter. A very
beautiful example by Fra Angelico is in
the Academy of Florence, in which St.
Peter is preaching to the Romans from
a pulpit, while St. Mark is seated and
reverently writes down the sermon in a
book. Another fine picture of the same
scene by Bonvicino is in the Brera, at
Milan.

Historical pictures of St. Mark are numerous, and are, as a rule, the works of
Venetian masters. Gentile Bellini, who
had been in the East, painted a picture
of St. Mark preaching at Alexandria, now
in the Brera. The scenery and costumes
are Oriental certainly, but they are Turk-

ish. Nothing Egyptian appears, either in the crowd of men and women which surrounds the platform on which the preacher stands, or in the background, in which a so-called church is essentially a mosque. The fact is that Bellini had been in Constantinople, but never in Egypt. It is surprising that this work should have been praised in Venice, where the incongruities of the composition must have been detected, since many Venetians had visited both Alexandria and Constantinople for commercial purposes.

The following legend is the subject of two famous pictures in the Academy of Venice, which cannot be understood without a knowledge of what they illustrate.

On the 25th of February, 1340, there was a great storm at Venice. The water had been rising during three days, and had reached a height of three cubits more than had ever been known before. An old fisherman had with great difficulty reached the Riva di San Marco, and determined to stay there until the storm ceased. But a man came to him and insisted that he should row to San Giorgio Maggiore. With difficulty the fisherman was persuaded to set out, and having reached San Giorgio the stranger landed, and ordered the boatman to await his return. When he came back to the boat he brought a young man with him, and commanded the fisherman to row to San Niccolo di Lido. The boatman doubted his ability to do this, but was assured that strength would be given him. Reaching the Lido, the two men landed and soon returned to the boat with a third. The fisherman was then told to row out beyond the two castles, and when at last they came to the sea they saw a barque filled with demons who were on their way to submerge the city.

The three strangers made the sign of the cross, and bade the demons depart. Instantly the barque vanished and the sea was calm. Then the fisherman was ordered to land each man at the place from which he had come, and when this was done, he demanded payment for his services of the last to land. The stranger replied, "Thou art right; go to the Doge and the Procuratori of St. Mark; tell them what thou hast seen. I am St. Mark, the protector of the city; the others were the brave St. George and the holy bishop, St. Nicholas. Tell them that the tempest was caused by a schoolmaster of San Felice, who sold his soul to Satan and then hanged himself." The fisherman replied that no one would believe his tale. Then St. Mark gave the man a ring, saying, "Show them this, and tell them that they will not find it in the sanctuary," and he disappeared. The next

morning the fisherman did as he was told,
and the ring could not be found in the
treasury of St. Mark. The fisherman was
paid, and a life pension was assigned him.
The ring was replaced by the Procuratori,
a grand procession was ordained, and with
great solemnity all Venice gave thanks to
God and the three saints for the preservation of the beautiful city.

In the beautiful and famous picture
in which Giorgione represented the storm,
a ship manned by demons is seen, and
they are evidently terrified. Some throw
themselves into the sea; some cling
to the flaming masts which cast a lurid
glare over the whole scene; others
hold fast to the rigging in sheer despera-
tion. Two barques are in the foreground,
that in which are the three saints, and
a second manned by four glowing red
demons. All over the sea are monsters
ridden by still other demons, and in the

distance the towers of Venice appear. Giorgione's poetic conception of the subject and his style of painting combine admirably in this work. His glowing colour and vigorous handling are here tempered by strong poetic feeling.

Paris Bordone chose a very different scene from the legend for his great work, which is considered his best large picture. He introduces to us a magnificent hall in which, on a dais, reached by a flight of steps, the Doge is seated in council. Hither comes the fisherman with the ring, which he holds out toward the Doge while ascending the steps. In spite of the gorgeous colour, the numerous figures, and the magnificent architecture of this picture, there is a certain simplicity and an air of truth about it, and its execution is more tender than was the customary manner of the famous Venetian painters.

Tintoretto illustrated still another legend of St. Mark, and his picture, also in the Academy, is world famous. A Christian slave, who persisted in worshipping at the shrine of St. Mark, is about to be tortured, when the saint descends from the sky, confounds the torturers, and destroys their implements. Of this picture Taine says: " No painting, in my judgment, surpasses, or perhaps equals, the St. Mark; at all events, no painting has made an equal impression on my mind. The saint descends from the uppermost sky head foremost, precipitated, suspended in the air. . . . No one, save Rubens, has so caught the instantaneousness of motion, the fury of flight; . . . we are borne along with, and follow, him to the ground, as yet unreached. Here, the naked slave, thrown upon his back, . . . glows with the luminousness of a Correggio. His superb, virile,

muscular body palpitates; . . . the axes
of iron and wood have been shattered to
pieces, without having touched his flesh,
and all are gazing at them. The tur-
baned executioner with upraised hands
shows the judge the broken handle with
an air of amazement. . . . The judge, in
a red Venetian pourpoint, springs half-way
off his seat and from his marble steps.
The assistants around stretch themselves
out and crowd up, some in sixteenth century armour, others in cuirasses of Roman
leather, others in barbaric simarres and
turbans, others in Venetian caps and dal-
matics, some with legs and arms naked,
and one wholly so, except a mantle over
his thighs and a handkerchief on his
head, with splendid contrasts of light and
dark, with a variety, a brilliancy, an inde-
scribable seductiveness of light reflected
in the polished depths of the armour,
diffused over lustrous figurings of silks,

imprisoned in the warm shadows of the
flesh, and enlivened by the carnations,
the greens, and the rayed yellows of the
opulent materials. Not a figure is there
that does not act, and act all over; not
a fold of drapery, not a tone of the body,
is there that does not add to the universal
dash and brilliancy. . . . There is no example of such luxuriousness and success
of invention. . . . I believe that, before
having seen this work, one can have no
idea of the human imagination," and so
on, page after page, Taine exalts the
genius of Tintoretto, who thus glorified
St. Mark.

It is certainly a fortunate circumstance
for the world that the bones of St. Mark
were brought to Venice. In what other
city would such a Basilica have been
raised above them, and in what other
school of art could this Evangelist have
been thus honoured?

St. Luke, like St. Mark, was not called by Christ, but was a disciple of St. Paul, with whom he journeyed to Rome, where he remained during the life of the great apostle, serving him with zeal and devotion.

There is some reason for believing that Luke had practised the healing art, since St. Paul called him "the beloved physician." The claim that he was an artist, however, rests on no early tradition, but on a later Greek legend, which can only be traced to the tenth century. Nevertheless, St. Luke is the chosen patron of painters, and is frequently represented in the act of painting the portrait of the Virgin Mary.

The most famous picture of this subject is in the Academy of St. Luke at Rome, and is attributed to Raphael. The saint kneels on a footstool before his easel, while the Virgin, with the child in her

MABUSE. — ST. LUKE PAINTING THE PORTRAIT OF
THE VIRGIN.

arms, is resting on clouds near him; she has a sweet expression of countenance, and the child seems to be very curious as to what the saint is doing. The ox is reposing behind St. Luke, and near it is a youthful figure — called that of Raphael — watching the progress of the artist.

A small picture of the same subject in the Grosvenor Gallery is also attributed to Raphael, but a lover of his art would unwillingly admit his authorship of these works. They lack the exquisite sentiment, the refinement of expression and of execution, which he must have exhibited in the painting of this poetic scene. In truth, while there is a picture of the same subject, by Van Eyck, in the Munich Gallery, which is quaint and unusual, and one by Aldegraef, in the Belvedere, and others in various public and private collections, I have seen none that seemed to me worthy of this motive, that fitly represented the exquisite condescension of the Virgin, or the rapturous inspiration which should have possessed the artist saint in her presence.

The picture by Mabuse, also in the Vienna Gallery, however, while it does not satisfy one's ideal, is very interesting. The scene is laid in a richly ornamented open porch, where St. Luke kneels before a desk, on which his canvas is laid; he holds his pencil, but an angel behind him guides his hand. The Virgin and Child appear on clouds sustained by three angels, while two others hold a splendid crown above her head. Nothing is omitted that could give the work a rich and luxurious aspect; the draperies on all the figures are abundant, and fall in heavy, graceful folds; even the angels are draped; the hair and veil of the Virgin are beautifully designed, and her position with the Child

— his hand caressing her face — is tender
and attractive.

The angel assisting St. Luke is a mar-
vel of drapery and splendid wings, and his
hair is in rows of curls, so regular and
unruffled that one is assured of the calm-
ness of the air through which he de-
scended to earth. St. Luke's dress is
more sombre than the angel's, but even
that is bordered with rich fur.

Every part of the architectural background is loaded with medallions and exquisite designs, and in an alcove is a statue
of Moses with the Tables of the Law,
mounted on an elaborate pedestal. This
work is a fine example of the period, the
end of the fifteenth century, and of the
Van Eyck school, to which Mabuse
belonged.

When one studies the costumes in the
pictures of Mabuse, a story that is told of
him does not seem improbable. It is that

when in the service of a nobleman who expected a visit from the Emperor Charles V., Mabuse, with other retainers, was given a rich silk damask for a costume to be worn on the occasion. Mabuse obtained the consent of his patron to his superintendence of the making of his own suit. The artist then sold the silk, and made a costume of paper which he painted to represent the damask so well as to perfectly deceive the nobleman. But some one told him of the trick, and he asked the emperor which of the suits pleased him most. Charles selected that of Mabuse, and would not believe that it was paper until he had touched it.

Of *St. John*, a near relative of the Saviour, and "the disciple whom Jesus loved," we have more knowledge than of the other Evangelists. A son of the fisherman Zebedee, a brother of James, a man of pure life and thought, of a sympathetic nature, he was one of the earliest followers of Christ; and ever after his discipleship began he was the constant and devoted companion of the Saviour so long as he remained on earth. It was John who was beside the Master at the Last Supper; who stood beside the cross when Jesus, in the solemn words, "Behold thy mother!" manifested his love and confidence in him; who placed the body of our Lord in the sepulchre; who witnessed the Transfiguration; and to the end of his life laboured for the spread of the religion that he loved.

He preached in Judea with St. Peter; he founded seven churches in Asia Minor; he was sent to Rome a prisoner, and is said to have been miraculously delivered from the boiling oil into which he was cast by his persecutors, who then accused him of sorcery, and confined him on Patmos, where, it is believed, he wrote his Revela-

tion. Being released from this exile, he
returned to his church at Ephesus, where
he wrote his Gospel when ninety years old,
and died a few years later.

So attractive is this Evangelist that he
is more frequently seen in works of art,
especially in devotional pictures, than are
the other three. He has also been more
frequently chosen as a patron saint. He
is represented, not only as an Evangelist
and saint, but also as a prophet.

In very ancient representations of this
Evangelist he appeared as an aged man;
gradually, however, he was pictured as
young, beardless, with flowing hair, and a
face expressive of absorbing and even
ecstatic inspiration. The eagle is always
near him, and when crowned with stars,
or having an aureole, is intended to symbolise the Holy Ghost. In some ancient
representations of St. John writing, the
eagle holds the pen or the ink; in other

pictures, when the saint is thus engaged, he gazes upward at a vision of the Madonna.

When St. John holds a sacramental cup from which a serpent issues, reference is made to the legend that in Rome, the cup from which he drank and which he presented to the communicants was poisoned, but did them no harm, the poison having passed from the cup in the guise of a serpent, while the poisoner fell dead at the feet of the saint. It is said that this attempt to take the life of St. John was commanded by the Emperor Domitian, who also sentenced him to death in boiling oil.

Another version is that St. John was challenged to prove the power of his faith by drinking of the poisoned cup, and that while the saint was unharmed the unbeliever fell dead before him.

The symbolism of the cup is also explained as referring to the words, "Ye shall drink indeed of my cup," and again, as commemorating the institution of the celebration of the Eucharist.

This Evangelist was a popular subject with the masters. A very beautiful representation is that of Correggio in the series of the Evangelists in the Cathedral of Parma. Domenichino seems to have delighted in multiplying pictures of St. John, as Guido did his Magdalens. His pictures were frequently more picturesque and æsthetic than spiritual, as in one of the most noted, now in the Brera. Here the saint, pen in hand, kneels before the Madonna, apparently in an ecstasy. Two little beings, who might personate cupids as appropriately as angels, are seen, one caressing the eagle, the other holding the cup with the serpent. This picture is admirably composed and executed, and is a good example of Domenichino's excellence in expression and colour.

RAPHAEL.—A GROUP FROM "LA DISPUTA."

There are pictures in which St. John
Baptist and St. John Evangelist are both
represented. They were kinsmen, both
were prophets, and the Evangelist was a
disciple of the Baptist before he became
a follower of Jesus. They appear in certain pictures of the Madonna, and I recall
the bas-relief on the tomb of Henry VII.
in Westminster Abbey, in which the contrast between the prophet of the wilderness and the beautiful Evangelist is most
effective. One of the most acceptable representations of the two Johns is in the
Church of Santa Maria-Sopra-Minerva, at
Rome. I do not know the sculptor of the
group which shows these saints as children
playing at the feet of the Madonna, as if
to amuse the Christ-child. The eagle of
the Evangelist is there, while the Baptist
has his reed-pipe.

Many historical pictures in which St.
John appears belong more appropriately

to the Life of Christ than to that of the saint, and do not come within my province here. They are often very beautiful, and St. John is easily recognised.

St. John in the Island of Patmos is usually represented as writing. He is seated on a rock or under a tree, in the midst of a desolate landscape, with the sea surrounding it. He looks at a vision of the Virgin in the clouds, while the eagle attends him, near at hand. This subject is usually one of a series illustrating his life in chapels dedicated to the Evangelist; it is also frequent in ancient manuscripts.

Carlo Dolci's picture of the Vision in the Island of Patmos, in the Pitti Gallery, is quite different from others. The saint kneels beside a rock, on which he rests his open book, and with his right hand raised to the vision, appears to be praying for her protection and aid. The Virgin is here without the child, a winged figure, with hands clasped as though she, in turn, were interceding for the saint. Below the vision is a horrible dragon — symbol of evil—apparently falling into the sea. Behind the saint, on a jagged rock, the eagle stands, with outspread wings, having an air of intense interest in the scene before him. The face and head of the aged saint are very beautiful and the hands are finely executed; the abundant and graceful drapery flowing out behind St. John serves to give a balance to the picture, and an element of comfort which somewhat lessens the effect of the desolation surrounding him.

To me, however, there is no picture of St. John, that I have seen, so satisfactory as that by Raphael, who introduces him in the midst of the prophets and apostles in his great picture of La Disputa, in the Vatican. The Evangelist here sits be-

tween Adam and David, apparently lost
to all else in writing his visions; his face
is one of the most beautiful and spiritual
among the many exquisite faces by this
great master.

There are several very interesting legends connected with this Evangelist, and
he is believed to have performed miracles
both before and after his death. Many
of these are celebrated in certain localities
only, and I know of no representations of
them to which I wish to refer, except one
which has been finely illustrated in a
chapel in Santa Maria Novella, in Florence, in a most effective fresco by Filippino Lippi. The legend runs that when
St. John returned from Patmos to Ephesus, he met a funeral cortège emerging
from the gate of the city, and on inquiry
learned that Drusiana had died, the woman
at whose house he had formerly lived.
The saint ordered the bier to be put

FILIPPINO LIPPI. — ST. JOHN THE EVANGELIST
RESTORING DRUSIANA TO LIFE.

down, and, when he had earnestly prayed, the woman was restored to life and returned with John to her house, where he again took up his abode.

Lippi's fresco is impressive and dramatic. In the background Ephesus is seen; in the middle ground is the city gate, of splendid architectural effect. In the centre of the foreground is the bier, on which Drusiana has risen to a sitting posture, while the aged Evangelist, touching her arm with one hand, raises the other toward heaven, calling on God to aid him in working this miracle.

A number of men and women watch the scene with intense interest, among whom the bearers of the bier are striking figures. The whole picture is very spirited. Critics have objected to some of the details, as that of a child alarmed by a dog, but the work is realistic and there is no feature that is not legitimate in a street scene.

In the niches on the exterior of the church of Or San Michele, in Florence, there are remarkable statues of the Evangelists, by famous sculptors. St. Matthew by Ghiberti; St. Mark by Donatello, before which Michael Angelo exclaimed, "Mark, why do you not speak to me?" St. Luke by Giovanni da Bologna; and St. John by Baccio da Montelupo.

CHAPTER III.

THE APOSTLES.

THE most ancient representations of the apostles, like those of the Evangelists, consist of symbols only; and these, in the most direct manner possible, express the thought that the disciples of Christ were, at first, the sheep over whom he, as a Shepherd, watched; and later, they, in their turn, became the shepherds who cared for those who were converted by the gospel which they were commanded to preach " to all nations."

In the most ancient representations of the apostles, in mosaics and pictures, Christ, as the Lamb of God, crowned with a nimbus, is raised on an eminence in the centre of the picture, while the

apostles are symbolised by twelve other
lambs, ranged on each side the central
figure.   The four rivers of Paradise flow
from the eminence on which the symbol
of Christ is placed, such rivers as St. John
described in Revelation, — "a pure river
of water of life, clear as crystal, proceeding
out of the throne of the Lamb of God;"
or such as Dante saw in the empyrean.

> . . . "I look'd
> And, in the likeness of a river, saw
> Light flowing, from whose amber-seeming waves
> Flash'd up effulgence, as they glided on
> 'Twixt banks, on either side, painted with spring,
> Incredible how fair: and, from the tide,
> There ever and anon, outstarting, flew
> Sparkles instinct with life; and in the flowers
> Did set them, like to rubies chased in gold."

In the study of Art there is great pleasure in thus tracing the same thought
through Scripture, poetry, and the so-
called Fine Arts.

In the representation of the Shepherd
and the Sheep, in Santa Maria-in-Traste-
vere, in Rome, six of the sheep come out
from Jerusalem, and six from Bethlehem.
There are examples in which the sheep
are entering the above cities, which probably represent converts rather than the
apostles themselves. Very rarely doves
were used as emblems of the apostles.

The lamb, as a symbol of the apostles,
may be significant of the office of Christ
as the Great Shepherd, or emblematical
of the deaths of the disciples, — slain like
sheep for his sake, — or may refer to the
texts of Scripture in which believers and
non-believers are likened to sheep and
goats, as in Matthew 25 : 32. Sheep and
lambs are used in other symbolic representations than those of the apostles, and
care is necessary in deciding upon their
significance in special cases.

The apostles were also pictured as

twelve men, each holding a sheep, with
Christ as the chief in the centre; in the
most ancient of these representations, the
faces were all alike. Again, they held
scrolls inscribed with their names, and
later the Apostles' Creed was used according to the tradition that each apostle contributed one of its propositions. Thus,
St. Peter, "I believe in God, the Father
Almighty, maker of heaven and earth;"
St. Andrew, "and in Jesus Christ, his
only Son, our Lord," and so on to the
end.

Figures of the apostles holding scrolls
inscribed with these sentences are seen
on the Tabernacle of the Church of Or
San Michele, in Florence.

After the sixth century each apostle
had a distinct symbol, and was easily distinguished by it. St. Peter rarely bears a
fish, the keys being far more frequently
given him. St. Paul has one, and, at

times, two swords. The transverse cross belongs to St. Andrew, and a pilgrim's staff is the symbol of St. James the Great; St. John, as an apostle, should have the chalice with the serpent, the eagle being his emblem as an evangelist. St. Thomas usually has a builder's rule, — more rarely, a spear; St. James Minor bears a club; and St. Philip has a cross in his hand, or bears a crosier ending in a cross; St. Bartholomew has a large knife, St. Matthew a purse, St. Simon a saw, St. Jude — or Thaddeus — a lance or halberd, and St. Matthias a lance.

The apostles are always represented as twelve in number, but the personality is varied in ancient mosaics and bronzes, in which they are sometimes presented according to the Byzantine rather than the Latin ritual. In some cases St. Paul replaces St. Jude, and there are examples in which SS. Mark and Luke are in-

cluded, to the exclusion of SS. Simon
and Matthias.

Statues of the apostles are used in
both the exterior and interior decoration
of churches, and could not be omitted
from any comprehensive system of ecclesiastical decoration. In many representations they are only superseded by Divine
Beings, according to the words of Christ:
" When the Son of Man shall sit in the
throne of his glory, ye also shall sit on
twelve thrones, judging the twelve tribes
of Israel."

The apostles by Jacobelli, on the top
of the choir screen in the Basilica of St.
 Mark, in Venice, and those by Peter
Vischer, on the tomb of St. Sebald, in
Nuremburg, — vastly different in treatment as are the Italian and German
schools which these statues represent, —
are the finest that I have seen where all
the Twelve are present. There are single

figures which I much prefer; for example, the St. James Major, by Thorwaldsen, in the *Frue Kirke*, in Copenhagen, and the St. Mark, on the exterior of Or San Michele, in Florence, already mentioned.

The apostles of Jacobelli and Vischer are in a sincere, unaffected style of religious art, far more devotional and acceptable than the dramatic groups of later date, such as Correggio painted in the churches of Parma. Picturesque and dramatic effects are unsuited to these single-hearted, fervent apostles, however artistically they may be handled.

The representation of the apostles in the fresco of the Last Judgment, in the Sistine Chapel, by Michael Angelo, and that by Raphael in La Disputa, in the Stanza della Segnatura, — both in the Vatican, — are most important in the history of Art. The first exhibits a company of undraped giants grouped about Christ

in his office of Judge of the World. They
are grand figures, demonstrating the great
master's marvellous powers of conception
and execution, and testifying to the val-
idity of his immortal fame, but one would
shrink from them as judges.

In the Disputa a number of the
apostles are omitted, the company including prophets and saints also. It is
an assemblage of great dignity, in which
the figures are fully draped, and seated on
clouds, on each side of the Three Persons
of the Trinity. They appear to be calmly
discussing the relations between God and
man, — the subject of the picture, which
is sometimes called " Theology." St.
Peter and others are easily distinguished
by their symbols. It is a most sympathetic representation of the " Communion
of Saints."

Pictures of the apostles in groups, in
historical, Scriptural, and legendary sub-

jects, are numerous and easily distinguished. Scenes from the life of Christ
in which they are present were favourite
motives with the masters, and the most
important subjects connected with them
after his death — the Descent of the Holy
Ghost, the Dispersion to Preach the Gospel, and the Twelve Martyrdoms — were
many times repeated. In these scenes
other figures are introduced; indeed, in
the wonderful representation of the Day
of Pentecost, in the chief dome of the
Basilica of St. Mark, — which consists of
several distinct parts, — there are not only
numerous figures, but fine architectural
features, a charming landscape with trees
and birds, and other effective details.
But the apostles, in whatever company
they appear, are distinguished by their
figures, their bearing, and the expression
of their faces, as well as by their symbols.

A volume would be required were one

to satisfactorily treat of the single figures
of the apostles in painting and sculpture,
and explain the historical or devotional
intention of such works.

In groups of apostles *St. Peter* is accorded the first place, by universal consent, and is frequently represented with
St. Paul and St. John the Evangelist.
SS. Peter and Paul are honoured, in old
mosaics especially, as founders and de-
fenders of the Christian Church in all the
world. Important examples of these are
seen in Santa Maria Maggiore, Santa
Sabina, and SS. Cosmo and Damian in
Rome; these belong to the fifth and sixth
centuries and are more curious and interesting than beautiful.

In the Cathedral of Monreale, at Pa-
lermo, the mosaic is of the twelfth century,
and is admirable. SS. Peter and Paul
are seated on magnificent thrones, the
former holding a book in one hand, and

VANDYCK. — ST. PETER.

two keys in the other, with which he gives the benediction. St. Paul has a book, and a sword with the point turned upwards. These ancient devotional representations are in a classical style of art, and the heads of the apostles are of the intellectual Greek type.

Milton, referring to St. Peter, says:

"Two massy keys he bore of metals twain,
  The golden opes, the iron shuts amain."

Dante, however, in the ninth Canto of Purgatory says: "Two keys of metal twain; the one was gold, its fellow silver," and these last are the metals usually represented in art.

The Deliverance of Peter from Prison, was an attractive subject to artists, and was many times represented, from the date of the early mosaics to the flowering time of religious art. In the mosaics in the Cathedral of Monreale, Peter sits on a stool, apparently much depressed, while the angel deliverer stands beside him.

Among the pictures of this subject the most famous are by Filippino Lippi, in the Brancacci Chapel in Florence, and by Raphael, in the Stanza di Eliodoro in the Vatican.

In the first scene of the Florentine frescoes, St. Peter looks through his grated window at St. Paul, who, with his right hand raised, is addressing the prisoner. This St. Paul is so grand a figure that Raphael found it a worthy model for his picture of St. Paul preaching at Athens. In the second scene the angel leads the apostle forth beyond the sleeping guard.

The St. Paul is perhaps the finest figure painted by Filippino, and the brilliant colouring adds to the splendid effect it produces. The angel and the sleeping sentry are also remarkably fine figures, although the colours have suffered, and are somewhat dull.

In Raphael's frescoes three scenes are devoted to this subject. In the first scene, Peter and two guards, to whom he is chained, are seen through a grating, all in a deep sleep; in the second scene a luminous angel has appeared and is leading Peter forth; in the third, the guards awaken, and are in consternation at the escape of the apostle.

The remarkable feature in these pictures is the effect of the light proceeding from the angel which illumines the first two scenes, in contrast with the light from the torch in the third scene. These works excited great and admiring enthusiasm in Italy, where the effects of varied lights had not been studied so carefully as in the Dutch and Flemish schools. Gerard Honthorst's picture of this very subject, in the Berlin Gallery, is a fine example of his school. This painter was called in Italy *Gerardo dalle Notti* — Gerard of the night — by reason of his painting of night scenes, and he is still called by this name in the history of painting.

Raphael indulged in a bold anachronism when he presented the guards of St. Peter in the steel cuirasses of his own time, and it has been thought that he intended this as an allusion to the escape of Leo X. after the battle of Ravenna, when he was made a prisoner by the French. As Leo was elected Pope on the first anniversary of his escape, Raphael very probably resolved that his fresco should commemorate that experience in the life of his patron.

The last of the eight famous pictures which Murillo painted for the Chàrity Hospital of Seville represents the release of St. Peter. It is now in the Hermit-

age in St. Petersburg. The composition
is quite different from those of which we
have spoken. Here, the apostle, seated
on the floor of his prison, is just awakened from sleep, and sees the beautiful
angel, from whom a glory of light proceeds. All the astonishment and pleasure which this vision must have brought
to the apostle are fully expressed in his
venerable face.

The Calling of SS. Peter and Andrew
is an interesting subject, and was represented by Basaiti in a work now in the
Vienna Gallery, and by Ghirlandajo in
the Sistine Chapel. Baroccio's picture of
this scene, in the Gallery of Brussels, is
also an excellent composition. Peter is
kneeling before Christ in the foreground;
the latter holds out his hand with a
welcoming gesture, as if saying, "Come
ye after me, and I will make you to become fishers of men." A little back of

Peter is his boat, over the side of which Andrew is climbing, while a man stands in the boat, holding it to the shore by pushing with a pole. The Sea of Galilee stretches away in the distance, and another small sailboat is seen.

There is a certain pathos in the face and pose of the Saviour, while Peter looks a stalwart, spirited man. Baroccio, though not a great artist, was correct in design, and skilful in his management of light and shade.

The numerous devotional pictures of St. Peter, as apostle and patron, with his key or keys, the book, and, occasionally, the cross, are too many to be spoken of in detail, and, as no other saint bears a key, he is at once recognised. When alone, and seated, he is represented in his office of Founder of the Church, — the Rock on which that Church was built. He usually has his hand raised

BAROCCIO. — THE CALLING OF ST. PETER AND
ST. ANDREW.

in benediction; he sometimes wears the triple tiara, as a Pope, and has always a commanding and earnest countenance.

The reference that has already been made to St. Mark, as the amanuensis of St. Peter, explains certain pictures in which they are in company. I have also referred to early representations in which SS. Peter and Paul are seen together; a peculiar significance was attached to such a composition, since Peter stood for the converted Jews, and Paul for the Gentiles, and together they represented the entire body of Christians. In a few cases the symbols are omitted, but the elder, robust man, with a short, thick beard, and sometimes a bald head, can scarcely fail to be recognised as Peter, beside the younger, smaller man, with the Greek type of face, the flowing beard, the high forehead, and singularly brilliant eyes. This representation is seen on ancient sarcophagi and in mosaics, rather than in pictures of a later time.

The various legends connected with St. Peter are nearly all depicted in St. Peter's, in Rome, but not in a manner that merits description. Those in the Brancacci Chapel — a portion of which we have mentioned — are finer than any other series from the life of this apostle. The subjects are both Scriptural and legendary. The Accusation of Peter and Paul before Nero is a remarkable work, and was not exceeded in dramatic composition before Raphael created his masterpieces, and that he studied these frescoes, and even modelled some of his figures after those he had seen here, is generally conceded. Nero is enthroned on the right of the scene, and is surrounded by ministers and attendants; Simon Magus, the accuser, and the apostles are in the foreground. Paul has an air of quiet dignity, while Peter, greatly excited, points with scorn to the shattered idol at his feet. All these figures are admirable; even Simon Magus is imposing, and, while there is a great variety in the expression of the faces, all are excellent.

It was a custom with the Florentine masters to introduce the portraits of prominent men and women into their frescoes, and it is probable that the pictures in the Brancacci Chapel contained many such likenesses, as did the frescoes by Ghirlandajo in the choir of Santa Maria Novella; but, unfortunately, the portraits of the Brancacci paintings cannot be identified as those by Ghirlandajo have been.

A beautiful legend runs that when Peter, at the solicitation of the Christians in Rome, was leaving the city to escape persecution, he was met by Christ; and when Peter asked our Lord whither he

was going, — *Domine, quo vadis?* — Jesus
replied, " I go to be crucified anew," and
vanished. Peter, understanding the re-
proof, returned .to Rome to meet his
death.

This scene has been but rarely painted.
I know of no good picture that represents
it. The only famous work of art associated with it is the statue of Christ in Santa
Maria-Sopra-Minerva in Rome, by Michael Angelo. It is supposed to represent
the Saviour when meeting Peter on the
Appian Way. It is not worthy the great
sculptor by whose name it is known ; its
faults may, however, be attributed to his
assistants in its execution rather than to
himself.

The picture of the *Domine, quo vadis*
in the National Gallery, London, by Anni-
bale Caracci, is far from satisfactory, and
that by Raphael — one of the small pictures in the Stanza della Torre Borgia,

ANDREA DEL SARTO. — ST. MICHAEL, ST. JOHN
GUALBERTO, ST. JOHN THE BAPTIST, AND
ST. BERNARD.

in the Vatican — is so comparatively insignificant as a work of this master as to merit slight attention.

In the Cappella degli Spagnuoli, in Santa Maria Novella, Florence, in a fresco by Simone Memmi, St. Peter is pictured as guarding the entrance to Paradise. He stands, a colossal figure, just within the gate, holding his key. On his left two angels place crowns of flowers on the heads of the accepted souls, who pass St. Peter in pairs, hand in hand.

Since the key is given to St. Peter only, he can never be mistaken when this symbol is present.

Although *St. Paul* was not a companion of Christ while on earth, he yet ranks next to St. Peter among the apostles. His life, well known by the Scripture account of him, especially by his own Epistles, serves to make him the most interesting of this important group of men. There are few legends connected with St. Paul, and a familiarity with the New Testament renders it easy to recognise the representations of him in Art.

His attribute, the sword, does not appear before the end of the eleventh century, and was not in general use until three centuries later, since which it is very rarely omitted. When he leans upon the sword his martyrdom is symbolised; when it is waved aloft it is an emblem of his intrepid warfare for Christianity. Very rarely two swords are given to St. Paul, as on the shrine of St. Sebald, by Peter Vischer, which treatment is explained as representing both his power — the usual meaning of his symbol — and his intrepidity.

In devotional pictures St. Paul is rarely seen alone, being usually accompanied by St. Peter or other apostles. Unfortunately, this saint appears in many mediocre pictures, as in those in the cupola of

St. Paul's in London, sketches of which may be seen in the vestry.

Hogarth's St. Paul before Felix, in Lincoln's Inn Fields, impressed me most unpleasantly. The figures are commonplace and coarse, while they have a certain force of personality, and are depicted with sufficient spirit to hold the attention for a time, and it must be praised for its admirable composition. But, on the whole, it is an undignified presentation of an important subject.

Guido Reni's picture of the Dispute at Antioch, now in the Brera, Milan, is famous among the pictures of St. Paul. Peter is seated with an open book on his knees, and is thoughtfully looking down; St. Paul stands opposite St. Peter, and regards him with an air of rebuke, as if saying, " When Peter was come to Antioch, I withstood him to his face, because he was to be blamed."

But all other pictures of this great apostle are unimportant when compared with Raphael's St. Paul preaching at Athens, one of the famous cartoons now in the South Kensington Museum, London. The grandeur of the composition, the life and action, the beauty of the figures and of the architecture, merit the celebrity this work has achieved. Passavant says:

"Amongst a numerous audience, St. Paul, standing on the steps, is announcing his divine message. His look and gestures are inspired, his whole bearing imposing. In the foreground Dionysius, the Areopagite, accompanied by his wife Damaris, is coming up the steps and testifying his enthusiasm. On the other side is a well-fed Epicurean, who seems very attentive, but still feels doubts; near him is a proud Stoic. The Sophists who are seated are already discussing the

words of St. Paul amongst themselves.
This masterly work is the image of the
first gigantic struggles of the Christian
Church, not yet with ignorance and bar-
barism, but with the whole pagan philoso-
phy and the worship of false gods."

In the St. Cecilia, in the Bologna Gallery, also by Raphael, the opposite side of
St. Paul's character is shown; here he is
as thoughtful — or as melancholy — as he
is spirited and grand when exclaiming,
" Whom ye ignorantly worship, Him I
declare unto you."

There is a difference of opinion as to
the fitness of Raphael's manner of representing St. Paul, the question being
whether the abundant hair and full beard
so well represents the ideal St. Paul, as
does the bald head and scanty beard given
him by other masters. If we remember
his toils and hardships, the preacher at
Athens does not suggest a man who has

survived such experiences ; but the living energy with which he addresses the
Athenians could scarcely be expected
from a worn and wasted traveller, who has
been "in weariness and painfulness, in
watchings often, in hunger and thirst, in
fastings often, in cold and nakedness."
Raphael was too thoughtful and too careful an artist to have thus represented the
apostle without a reason satisfactory to
himself.

St. Andrew is distinguished in works of
art by his transverse cross, and when fastened to it he is bound with cords, according to the legend of his death. Very few
subjects connected with this apostle are
represented in pictures, and are so painful
that they would not be noticed except for
great excellence in conception and execution ; they are his Adoration of his Cross
before being bound to it, his Flagellation,
and his Death.

The chapel of Sant' Andrea in the Church of San Gregorio, Rome, was decorated by Guido Reni and Domenichino. Guido painted the Adoration of the Cross, and Domenichino, the Flagellation, and in Sant' Andrea - della - Valle Domenichino represented the Flagellation, the Crucifixion, and the Apotheosis of St. Andrew. Guido's picture is disappointing in view of the fact that, with those of Domenichino, it has been accorded some importance in the history of Art. The others are fine in colour, and the groups of women and children who witness these scenes are well composed, and fitly express their fright and horror. Some critics have gone so far as to say that, had these figures power to speak, they could say no more than they now express.

In the Pitti Gallery is Carlo Dolci's martyrdom of St. Andrew, which admirably expresses the devotional spirit of the saint, who knelt before his cross and saluted it as precious, since the crucifixion of Jesus had consecrated all crosses. The modelling of the hands is especially fine in this picture.

So important is St. Andrew as a patron saint that one might reasonably look for many pictures of him. In the fourth century portions of his relics were taken to Scotland, and he was made the protector of that country and of its chief Order of chivalry. Other relics of the saint were brought to Burgundy, and the Order of the Golden Fleece, so important in Flanders and Spain, was placed under the care of St. Andrew, while he was still further exalted as patron of the Russian Order of the Cross of St. Andrew.

I know of no picture of this apostle by any Flemish or German artist that merits attention. In Spain, Roelas painted a martyrdom of St. Andrew, now in the

Provincial Museum of Seville, which is one of the famous pictures of the Seville school. This artist had studied medicine before he became a painter, and his anatomical knowledge was very valuable in representing subjects of this nature, which are most painful.

But Murillo's picture of the same subject, in the Museum of Madrid, is the finest representation of St. Andrew that I have seen. Of necessity it is a distressing picture, but the two angels, — beautiful as Murillo's angels are, — bringing from heaven the crown and palm, are reminders of Christian hope and joy, such as are entirely wanting in the works of Guido and Domenichino. The saint, too, appears to feel their influence, and gazes at the heavenly messengers with an expression of holy exultation. While supremely tragic in effect, this picture has a poetic element which tempers its intense sadness.

St. James the Great — St. James Major — is presented in Scripture as a favourite follower of Our Lord, and was present at many of the scenes described in the Gospels. Although he slept through the Agony in Gethsemane, he had been one of the three permitted to witness the Transfiguration of Christ. After the Ascension, we read only of his being slain by Herod.

St. James is celebrated as the first disciple who went forth to preach the gospel. For this reason he is represented in a pilgrim's dress, and even when the cloak, hat, gourd, and scallop-shell are omitted, he retains the pilgrim staff, and may thus be recognised in pictures of the Madonna and other scenes in which saints are grouped.

The statue of St. James by Thorwaldsen, in the *Frue Kirke* in Copenhagen, already mentioned, is very beautiful, and so full of life and motion that, when at a little distance, and having a side view of it, one watches to see it take the step that the sculptor must have arrested.

In many representations of St. James Major, a resemblance to the usual face and figure of Christ is distinctly noticeable, and indicates his near human relationship to Jesus.

Andrea del Sarto painted a beautiful picture of St. James — now in the Uffizi Gallery — as a standard for the *Compagnia di Sant' Jacopo*. Processional standards were of such importance to the confraternities that the best artists were employed to paint them, even the Madonna di San Sisto having been painted for this purpose. Del Sarto represented St. James with two children at his feet, one with hands clasped as if asking a benediction from the saint, who, reaching down, puts his hand beneath the boy's chin in an assuring and caressing manner.

As patron saint of Spain St. James is very important, and, according to the Spanish legends, the humble follower of Jesus was not a fisherman, but a young noble who used his boats for pleasure, and who, after the Ascension, became a great warrior and led the Spaniards to their victory over the Moors. Especially did he aid the army of King Ramirez, when he refused to deliver the annual tribute of a hundred Christian maidens to the Moorish sovereign. The legend recounts that at the famous battle of Clavijo the saint appeared on a milk-white steed, waving aloft a snow-white banner; sixty thousand Moors were slain, and this battle having given Spain a decisive victory, from that date, A. D. 939, the Spanish war-cry has been *Santiago !*

There are numerous Spanish legends

connected with St. James which are scarcely worth repetition, and but few pictures illustrating them are known to me.

In a chapel of the Church of St. Anthony at Padua, there is a series of sixteen pictures, executed in the fourteenth century, illustrating the life of this saint.

A very famous picture of Santiago was painted by Carreño de Miranda, for the high altar of Santiago. It is spirited and grand, and represents the saint as he is said to have appeared at Clavijo, riding a powerful white charger; he holds his banner in one hand, and his sword in the other, with which he is cutting down the Moors, the ground being already thickly strewn with their bodies. The saint's head is bare; his cloak, raised by the wind, flutters behind him.

As *St. Philip* was one of the first disciples called by the master, one would think that he would appear frequently in works

of art. On the contrary, there are few
pictures of him. In fact, I have seen but
one that has left any impression on my
memory. This is by Bonifazio, and is
in that treasure-house, the Academy of
Venice. Here St. Philip is before the
Saviour in an attitude of supplication.
Other apostles are in the background.
The picture is explained by the inscription, "Lord, show us the Father, and it
sufficeth us," and the answer, "Philip, he
that hath seen me hath seen the Father;
I and the Father are one."

This work is splendid in colour, as deep
and rich as Titian's, whom Bonifazio imi-
tated, although he was a student with the
elder Palma. His works are a striking
example of the result of patient industry
without the aid of unusual talent.

Occasionally one sees a statue of St.
Philip. In one of the niches on the exterior of Or San Michele, in Florence, is

his statue by Nanni di Banco; another, by Beccafumi, is on the Cathedral of Siena; and a figure of the apostle, seated and reading, by Ulrich Mair, is in the Belvedere in Vienna.

St. Bartholomew is rarely seen in works of art. In pictures, he usually appears in groups of apostles, and is sometimes made most unattractive by his emblem of his own skin, he having been flayed before his crucifixion; and when, added to this, he carries a large knife, he more nearly resembles a slayer from the shambles than a saint. He is thus represented in the Last Judgment, by Michael Angelo, in the Sistine Chapel.

Ribera apparently found the martyrdom of St. Bartholomew a subject suited to his art, since he painted it more than once, with a sickening fidelity to its details, and also made an etching of it. One of these pictures is in the Pitti Gallery, a second in the Pinacothek at Munich, and a third in the museum at Madrid.

The statue of this apostle, in the Milan Cathedral, has the same repulsive symbols. It is remarkable for its fine anatomy, and for its Latin inscription, which boastfully announces that its author was not Praxiteles, but Marco Agrati.

Tradition teaches that St. Bartholomew was an Egyptian prince, and among the statues recently placed on the façade of the cathedral in Florence, there is an impressive, dignified statue of the saint in Oriental costume. The full, flowing drapery, and the artistic head-dress produce an admirable contour, and the whole figure is imposing in effect. I saw it in the studio of Signor Fantacchiotti before it was raised to its present position, and consider it the best representation of St. Bartholomew of which I know.

St. Thomas, the doubting disciple, was

of an impulsive and affectionate nature as was shown in his desire to die with the Saviour, expressed in St. John 11 : 16, and 20 : 25. Tradition teaches that he preached the gospel in India, and from a legend connected with that country the builder's rule is his symbol, while in pictures the fruit and flowers of the Orient refer to the same spiritual and lovely legend. This relates that Jesus appeared to St. Thomas and desired him to go to India to build a palace for King Gondoforus. After giving his commands to Thomas, the king gave him an enormous amount of money to use in building the palace, and went away for two years. Thomas built nothing and distributed the money to the poor. Returning, the king cast Thomas into prison and sentenced him to a terrible death.

But a brother of the king, who had died, appeared to Gondoforus, and assured him that in Paradise the angels had shown him a splendid palace which they said Thomas had built for Gondoforus. Then the king liberated the saint, who said: "Knowest thou not, O king, that in heaven there are rich palaces for those who purchase them by faith and earthly charity. Thy riches may prepare for thee the way to such a place, but they cannot follow thee thither."

On account of this legend St. Thomas is the patron saint of architects, and as portions of his remains were found by the Portuguese at Meliapore and transported to Goa, he is the patron saint of their country; he is also the protector of Parma, where, in the fresco of the Assumption, in the cathedral, Correggio has introduced a fine picture of him.

The chief historical subject in the life of St. Thomas is the Incredulity, or his doubt of the death and resurrection of

Christ, which was satisfied only by actual contact with the wounds of the Saviour. This incident is represented either at the moment when the apostle is examining the wounds, or when, having done so, he is in an attitude of adoration, gazing heavenward with an expression of wonder and love.

Vandyck pictured the saint as examining the wounded hand, while in the splendid picture by Rubens, in the Antwerp Gallery, the apostle has his hand on the side of the risen Christ, while his face expresses astonishment and grief. SS. Peter and John are near by, and the whole work is most satisfactory; I know of no other picture of the doubting Thomas that approaches it in excellence. Guercino's picture in the Vatican Gallery has been much admired, but the position of Christ and the saint, both seen in profile, lessens the effect of the scene when compared with that of Rubens.

The picture known as the Madonna of the Girdle illustrates the legend that when the Virgin Mary ascended to heaven in the sight of the apostles, St. Thomas was absent, and on his return could not believe the wonderful story of her translation. Then the Virgin, pitying his doubting state, as her son had done, threw her girdle down to him, while appearing in the clouds above. By reason of this legend the girdle is sometimes placed in the hand of the apostle instead of his usual symbol, the builder's rule.

This subject was popular with the Florentine painters, as it was believed that this heaven-sent girdle was preserved in the neighbouring Cathedral of Prato.

The composition of Granacci's picture, in the Uffizi, is exquisitely simple and acceptable. The Virgin appears in the clouds, surrounded by angels. Beneath her is the tomb from which she has risen, now

F. GRANACCI. — THE MADONNA OF THE GIRDLE.

filled with flowers. St. Thomas kneels on one side of the tomb and clasps the girdle which the Virgin lets down to him, while he gazes at her in adoration; St. Michael kneels on the other side, with his face turned to the spectator, as if to say, "Observe this miraculous event, and let your faith be strengthened."

In the chapel of the *Sacra Cintola* — Sacred Girdle—in the Cathedral of Prato, the Assumption of the Virgin, by Agnolo Gaddi, about 1395, shows St. Thomas in the lower part, stretching out his arms for the girdle which Mary is loosening from her person. This fresco is one of the best preserved works of this most famous pupil of Giotto.

St. James Minor is rendered interesting by the legend that he so resembled Jesus —who was his first cousin—that the kiss of Judas was necessary in order that James should not be mistaken for Our

Lord. In ancient pictures this resemblance is so pronounced that he would be easily recognised without his symbol, the fuller's club, which typifies the manner of his death. He has not been a favourite saint and there are no pictures of him so important as to demand description. In devotional pictures he leans on his club, and sometimes carries a book.

Neither do *St. Simon Zelotes*, nor *St. Jude*, also called Thaddeus, merit special attention in Art, the pictures of them are so few. The symbol of St. Simon is a saw, and that of St. Jude a halberd, both symbolic of the manner of their martyrdom.

In this connection, however, a picture by Perugino, in the museum at Marseilles, should be mentioned. It is called a Holy Family, and it is claimed that every relative of Christ named in the Scripture is here represented. At the feet of the enthroned Virgin are two lovely children on whose aureoles the names Simon and Thaddeus are written.

The Scripture warrant for such a picture — Matthew 13 : 55, and Mark 15 : 40 — is so full that one wonders that it was not painted frequently, and while Perugino's work is good, a more spiritual and imaginative artist than he would have found a deeper inspiration in it.

St. Matthias, who was called to replace the traitor Judas, is rarely seen in pictures of groups of the apostles, and as rarely in a devotional picture alone. The Germans make his symbol an axe, while the Italians give him a lance.

One cannot speak of *Judas* as a saint, and is sorry to associate him with the apostles, and yet he appears in pictures which cannot be ignored. He is very properly introduced in several scenes in the life of Christ, and is easily recognised.

When represented as extremely repulsive in person it seems to me an error, since it would not seem that one whose very face revealed so hateful a character could have been chosen or retained as an apostle. The legends represent him as a comely person, and Fra Angelico, in his picture of Judas receiving the thirty pieces of silver, now in the Academy of Florence, has made him well featured, with a wicked expression.

So in Perugino's picture of the Magdalen anointing the feet of the Saviour,  in the Academy of Venice, the face of Judas expresses anger at the waste of the precious ointment, but he is well featured, and only ugly in expression.

In early Italian art one meets with a horrible nightmare style of representing Judas, which is not surprising when one recalls those lines in the thirty-fourth canto of Dante's Inferno, which describe

the agonies of Judas in one of Lucifer's
three horrid mouths.

"At every mouth his teeth a sinner champ'd,
   Bruised as with ponderous engine; so that three
   Were in this guise tormented.   But far more
   Than from that gnawing, was the foremost pang'd
   By the fierce rending whence oft-times the back
   Was stripp'd of all its skin.   'That upper spirit,
   Who hath worst punishment,' so spake my guide,
   'Is Judas, he that hath his head within
   And plies the feet without.'"

CHAPTER IV.

THE FATHERS OF THE CHURCH.

IN important religious decorations the Fathers, or Doctors of the Church, follow the Evangelists and apostles, and are sometimes grouped with them, as is fitting when we regard the Evangelists and apostles as the spiritual forces of the Church, and the Fathers as those who, in the Church Militant, contended, even through great sorrow and suffering, for what they conceived to be the only creed that embodied the true faith of the Christian Church.

There are few, if any, representations of the Fathers that accord them the full honour due their office and their labours

134

before the tenth century, the period when their importance and their sanctity was fully acknowledged, — when their teaching was regarded as infallible, and they, in short, believed to be inspired by God.

The Latin Fathers are those of the Western Church, — SS. Jerome, Ambrose, Augustine, and Gregory, better known as Gregory the Great. These are more familiar in works of art than are the Greek Fathers, or those of the Eastern Church, — SS. John Chrysostom, Basil the Great, Athanasius, and Gregory Nazianzen, to whom St. Cyril of Alexandria is frequently added.

When the Latin Fathers are represented in a group, *St. Jerome* is sometimes in a cardinal's dress and hat, although cardinals were not known until three centuries later than his time, but as the other Fathers held exalted positions in the Church, and were represented in ecclesiastical costumes, and as St. Jerome held a dignified office in the court of Pope Dalmasius, it seemed fitting to picture him as a cardinal. The Venetian painters frequently represented him in a full scarlet robe, with a hood thrown over the head. When thus habited, his symbol was a church in his hand, emblematic of his importance to the universal Church.

St. Jerome is also seen as a penitent, or again, with a book and pen, attended by a lion. As a penitent, he is a wretched old man, scantily clothed, with a bald head and neglected beard, a most unattractive figure. When he is represented as translating the Scriptures, he is in a cell or a cave, clothed in a sombre coloured robe, and is writing, or gazing upward for inspiration. In a few instances, an angel is dictating to him.

St. Ambrose is represented in his bishop's robe with mitre and crosier, carrying his book also ; again, he carries a knotted scourge, and a beehive is frequently placed near him.

St. Augustine has a variety of symbols; he is habited as a bishop and carries a book, while other books are at his feet or by his side ; sometimes his emblem is a flaming heart, pierced by an arrow.

As a Pope, *St. Gregory* has the tiara and the crosier with the double cross. His special attribute is the dove ; in ancient pictures this symbol is never far from his ear, sometimes apparently whispering to him, or hovering about his head and shoulders.

Although the Greek Fathers preceded the Latin Fathers as teachers, pictures of them are rarely seen except in Byzantine art. The schism between the Greek and Latin Churches engendered a bitterness which survived for centuries, and Latin artists seem to have forgotten that at one period all the Fathers belonged to all the Church.

The Greek Fathers have a common symbol, a scroll, or book, and the name of each one is inscribed near him. Almost without exception, the right hand is raised in the Greek form of benediction, — the first and second fingers extended, and the third finger and thumb joined, so that a cross is made on the inside of the hand. The scrolls in the hands of the Greek Fathers are inscribed with important sentences from their writings.

A good example of the introduction of the Fathers in important ecclesiastical decoration is seen in Correggio's fresco in the dome of the Church of San Giovanni, in Parma, in which they are seated near the Evangelists.

The Fathers are also introduced in important scenes in the life of Christ, and in that of the Virgin. In the academy at

Venice is a very interesting picture of the
Virgin Enthroned, by two of the Vivarini,
a family of painters who flourished in the
middle of the fifteenth century, and were
also called Da Murano, having been born
on that island. This picture is attributed
to Giovanni and Andrea da Murano. The
Virgin is enthroned beneath a baldachin,
or canopy, supported by four angels, and
apparently placed in the centre of a garden. The throne is on an ornamental
platform, slightly elevated, with an elaborate architectural screen behind it, beyond
which the tops of trees appear. The Holy
Child stands on the Virgin's knee, and on
each side, at a little distance, are two
Fathers, — SS. Jerome and Gregory on the
right, SS. Ambrose and Augustine on
the left.

This picture is overloaded with ornament, and has what has been called an
" admirable serenity of colour; " it is an

excellent example of the usual method of
representing the Latin Fathers.   Even
at the early date of its execution, the
Venetian characteristics were well pronounced.   The generous, ornamental draperies, the well-conditioned angels and
rosy-cheeked Madonna, the venerable bald
heads and flowing beards, as well as the
gorgeousness of colour, are more than
suggested in the works of the Muranese.
I know of no Venetian painting of the
same period which excels this in interest
and excellence.

There are many pictures which resemble
this Virgin Enthroned, in subject and
arrangement, and the Fathers can scarcely
be mistaken in such works, or when com-
muning together over the theological
mysteries which interested them.   In the
latter representations there is frequently
a heavenly vision which is apparent to
one or two, but not to all the Fathers.

ANDREA DEL SARTO. — ST. AUGUSTINE INSTRUCTING
ST. DOMINIC, ST. PETER MARTYR, ST. LAW-
RENCE, ST. SEBASTIAN, AND ST. MARY
MAGDALENE.

Good examples of this treatment are Guido's picture in the Hermitage at St. Petersburg, and that by Dosso Dossi, in the Dresden Gallery.

Pictures of St. Jerome are more numerous than those of the other Doctors of the Church. Especially is this true of the devotional pictures in which he is alone. The reasons for this are not far to seek; he not only translated the scripture, but he was the founder of monastic life in the West; he passed four years in penance in the desert, the awful sufferings of which time are known from his own account of them; he was a man of varied attainments, as well as a Christian who waged a continual warfare against everything that was not in harmony with a life consecrated to the service of Christ; all of which raised him to an exalted position in the Church.

The engravings and wood-cuts of St.

Jerome writing or translating, by Albert Dürer, are rare, but exist in a few collections, and, to my mind, excel all other representations of this subject. That of St. Jerome in his Chamber is a copperplate, and is esteemed as one of Dürer's three best engravings. It is very brilliant and minutely finished in every part. The saint is writing at his desk; the room, lighted by two arched windows, is cheerful with sunshine, and the venerable head, with its white halo, fixes the interest of the scene where it should be. To the sleepy lion and drowsy watch-dog in the foreground, Dürer added some characteristic German accessories; a pumpkin hangs from a beam, and various useful utensils divide the attention of the spectator with the learned-looking codices near the saint.

Pictures of St. Jerome as a penitent were painted for the Jeronymites, who claim St. Jerome as their founder. The edifices of this order are remarkable for their magnificence, and these pictures are too numerous to be spoken of in detail. St. Jerome is essentially the typical male penitent, as Mary Magdalene is the female, and in this view these saints are most important.

Titian's St. Jerome Penitent, now in the Brera, Milan, was painted for the Duke of Mantua in 1563, and is first among the representations of this subject, painful as it is. It represents a wild, mountainous country, in the centre of which the saint kneels on a rock, and gazes at a cross fixed above him. He is nude but for a scanty drapery about the loins, and holds in his hand the stone with which he beats his breast; the lion sleeps in the foreground; a skull and hour-glass are on a rock at the right, together with two clasped volumes. The effect of this picture is marvellously powerful. If one studies it seriously he is transported to a desolate solitude, dedicated to repentance, chastisement, and self-inflicted horrors, the effects of which are all too manifest in the emaciated body and the apparent wretchedness of this famous penitent. It is supremely suited to the purpose for which it was painted.

Almost every Italian artist of note represented this subject, and one only needs to see the Spanish pictures in any gallery — but especially in the Louvre — to discern that its mysticism and gloom rendered it most attractive to the painters of Spain.

One of the famous pictures of the world is the Last Communion of St. Jerome, by Domenichino. It is honoured with a position near the Transfiguration, by Raphael, in the Vatican Gallery. The scene is the porch of the chapel of a monastery,— as he commanded that he should be borne to the chapel at Bethlehem, just

before his death, — through the open arch
of which a lovely landscape is seen. The
dying saint, supported by his disciples,
kneels before the ecclesiastic, who presents the wafer to him, while one attendant
priest holds the cup, and a second, kneeling, bears the book and taper. The body
of the saint is painfully emaciated, but the
aureole is already about his head, and
there is comfort in the thought that, as
soon as the viaticum is received, the soul
will be freed from the sufferings of the
flesh.

The lion is near the feet of the saint;
above is a group of four angels who watch
the solemn scene. The woman, partly
concealed by the vestments of the priest,
who kisses the hand of the saint, is his
faithful disciple, St. Paula, a noble Roman
matron who followed St. Jerome to Bethlehem and there built a monastery, a
hospital, and three nunneries.

Jerome's visit to Rome was fruitful in the conversion of women of patrician blood, of wealth, intellect, and beauty. Not only St. Paula, but her daughter Eustochium, and her granddaughter Paula, became members of the community established by St. Paula at Bethlehem, the austerities of which were so severe that even St. Jerome disapproved of them.

The first book of Mrs. Oliphant's Makers of Rome gives a comprehensive sketch of the personality and influence of St. Jerome, in a charming manner.

There are several statues of St. Jerome that merit notice. That by Torrigiano, in the museum at Seville, is famous; it represents the saint as kneeling on a rock with a crucifix in one hand, and the stone of torture, with which he was accustomed to beat himself, in the other. The statue of St. Jerome in the Frari, in Venice, by Alessandro Vittoria, is said to be a por-

trait of Titian when ninety-seven years old;
there is something about it that does not
indicate the penitent, although the stone
is in his hand, and the lion at his feet.
Several other statues of St. Jerome are
seen in Venice, but are like a patron saint
rather than a penitent, and represent a
very different spirit from that of the saint
in Titian's wonderful picture.

St. Ambrose was an ideal "muscular
Christian," and his symbol of the knotted
scourge of three thongs is a suitable emblem of his punishment of the Emperor
Theodosius, and his unsparing condemna-
tion of sins committed by the people of
his cure.

A picture in the Frari, at Venice, presents St. Ambrose making good use of
his scourge, as, mounted on a spirited
horse, he flourishes it as if to strike down
all Arians who are not trampled by his
steed. Most of the pictures of this Father

represent his stern warfare against the followers of Arius, whom he hated inexpres-
sibly, and pursued with zeal.

His chapel in the Frari contains a
grand picture by Luigi Vivarini and
Marco Basaiti. Here the Father is enthroned in all the state which pertained
to his office as bishop. Even here the
scourge is in his hand, and he looks the
uncompromising foe to heretics that we
know him to have been. A glorious company of saints surround his throne, in
which are the other Latin Doctors, all
appearing to defer to St. Ambrose as to
a leader and superior.

On the steps of the throne are two
musical angels, most suitably placed, since
Ambrose gave great attention to music,
and to him we owe the introduction of the
manner of chanting the service, known as
the Ambrosian chant.

Basaiti gave a brilliant colour to his

pictures, and finished them carefully; these characteristics are seen in the works of the Vivarini in which he was associated, but the broad, fine lines, and the bold sweep of the perspective, as well as the excellent grouping of the saints in this picture, are due to Luigi Vivarini; this reflection deepens the regret that he did not live to complete this work, which fell into the hands of less artistic associates.

In the wonderful Basilica of Sant' Ambrogio Maggiore, in Milan, which was founded by St. Ambrose, and dedicated to all the saints, the incidents in the life of this Father are depicted in silver gilt relief, on the back of the altar. Curiously, as it would seem, the violent scenes — those which warrant the use of the scourge as his symbol — are omitted. Even his expulsion of Theodosius from this same basilica is not represented.

In the Belvedere, Vienna, a picture by

Rubens shows the scene when the Father refused to permit the Emperor to enter the cathedral. This was a subject well suited to the great Flemish master, and he did it full justice. A very beautiful small copy of this picture, by no less an artist than Vandyck, is in the National Gallery.

The scene is the porch of the cathedral; on the steps is Theodosius, surrounded by his attendants; his attitude is that of hesitating supplication. Above is St. Ambrose, with several priests, who stretches out his hand toward the emperor in a forbidding manner.

In recent times St. Charles Borromeo is sometimes represented with St. Ambrose, partly because he was Archbishop of Milan, and partly on account of his tomb which is in this basilica.

St. Augustine is very important among the Doctors of the Church, and the con-

stant use of his beautiful Te Deum causes
him to be held in grateful remembrance.
He composed this for the occasion of his
baptism by St. Ambrose, in the Cathedral
of Milan, and its first recital — when the
two saints advanced to the altar, each re-
peating the alternate verses of this grand
hymn of praise — would seem to furnish a
subject to be welcomed by artists. Pictures of the baptism are seen in chapels
dedicated to St. Augustine, but I have
seen none which emphasise the introduction of the Te Deum.

The restless, and even dissipated, youth
of this Father gave little promise of such
a life as he led in later years, nor could it
be reasonably imagined that his theological writings should be so numerous and
become so celebrated as to lead scholars
and theologians to look to him as their
patron saint.

Pictures of St. Augustine alone are

rare. He has no special symbol, and simply appears as a bishop. When such a figure with a pen or a book is seen in company with St. Jerome, it is probably St. Augustine. He is, however, usually represented with groups of saints, among whom his mother, St. Monica, is frequently seen. A fine picture of this type, by Andrea del Sarto, is in the Pitti Gallery. St. Augustine is represented as speaking, in his office of Doctor of Theology; SS. Dominic, Francis, and Lawrence listen attentively, while Mary Magdalene and St. Sebastian kneel in the foreground. Del Sarto reached an elevated style in painting; his composition was fine, his draperies graceful and harmonious, the whole feeling of his works tranquil, and, as a whole, they make an impression of having been easily and simply conceived and executed. He can be well studied in the Pitti.

Of this picture of St. Augustine, Kugler says: "St. Augustine is speaking with the highest inspiration of manner; St. Dominic is being convinced with his reason, St. Francis with his heart; St. Lawrence is looking earnestly out of the picture, while St. Sebastian and the Magdalene are kneeling in front, listening devoutly. We here find the most admirable contrast of action and expression, combined with the highest beauty of execution, especially of colouring."

The Ecstasy of St. Augustine, when, borne aloft by angels, he beheld the Saviour, was painted by both Murillo and Vandyck, and both introduced the kneeling figure of St. Monica. Murillo's picture is in the Museum of Madrid; Vandyck's made a part of a private gallery in England.

A picture frequently seen and known as the Vision of St. Augustine illustrates the legend that, as the saint walked on the seashore, he saw a child who, having dug a hole in the sand, was filling it with water. When the saint asked the child what he did, the child replied that he intended to pour all the water of the sea into this hole. When the saint assured him that such a task could never be finished, the child replied, " It is no more impossible to do this than for thee to comprehend and explain the mystery on which thou art meditating ! "

One is surprised that this subject has been so many times painted. It is not especially attractive, and suggests no deep sentiment. A bishop appears to be advising a child as to his manner of making a mud pie. If one does not know the legend it is extremely commonplace, and when it is known the picture has no spirituality. Murillo made the most attractive picture of it that I know, but the subject seems

GAROFALO. — THE VISION OF ST. AUGUSTINE.

unworthy of his brush; it is now in the Gallery of the Louvre.

There is a picture of this Vision by Garofalo, in the National Gallery. St. Augustine is seated on one side of the beach, where his books are laid on a rock before him. Behind him is St. Catherine, and they regard the beautiful child attentively. He is beside his hole on the sand, and points to the sea, which he intends to pour into it. In the distance, on the beach, is the figure of an ecclesiastic, said to represent St. Stephen. Beyond the stretch of water a varied landscape is seen, and in the clouds is a vision of the Madonna and Child, with numerous angels, some of whom are playing on musical instruments.

Vandyck and Rubens also painted pictures of this Vision, but even their genius failed to impart mysticism or poetry to the scene. Vandyck's picture

is in the Church of St. Augustine, in
Antwerp.

The tomb of St. Augustine, in the
Cathedral of Pavia, is the most magnificent and interesting work of art connected
with his name. Its author is unknown,
but it is attributed with some authority
to Bonino da Campiglione, and is said to
have been begun in 1362. It is possible
that Cicognara and the Jacobelli were
employed on it. There might well have
been a small army of sculptors engaged
in the work, since it is embellished with
two hundred and ninety figures. The
story of St. Augustine's life is told in
bas-reliefs. There are many statues
of important saints, as well as those
of the Evangelists and apostles. The
effigy of the saint lies on a bier, and
exquisitely beautiful angels are folding
the grave clothes about it. Six centuries have but slightly discoloured the

fine, white marble of which this tomb is made.

St. Gregory, both saint and pope, better known as Gregory the Great, was of a patrician family, and his mother, while he was still an infant, was impressed by a dream, or vision, with a firm belief that her son would be a Pope. She accordingly endeavoured to fit him by his education for the exalted office of the Head of the Church.

Until his father's death, however, Gregory was a lawyer by profession, but when he came into his inheritance he devoted himself to charities, and founded a monastery and hospital.

When his predecessor, Pope Pelagius, died, Gregory refused to be made Pope, but was forced by the will of the Church, the people, and the emperor, — for all these were in accord, — to accept this exalted office, in which he became famous in various directions.

Gregory was the first to preach the doctrine of purgatory; he it was who instituted
the celibacy of the clergy, who first sought
to Christianise England, who carefully
regulated the forms for church services,
arranged the music of the chants known
by his name, and superintended the in-
struction of priests and choristers in order
that they should properly conduct themselves, and teach the people decency and
order in worship.

In short, there have been few Popes,
indeed few men in any position, whose
influence has been so far-reaching, in so
many avenues, as that of Gregory the
Great, and few whose lives are more interesting than his. The story of his seeing
the Saxon children in Rome, and under-
taking to Christianise England, that of
the processions organised by him to pray
for the stay of the plague, and the vision
of the archangel sheathing his sword above

the tomb of Hadrian, and many of his works as priest, monk, and Pope, present him to us as a man of wonderful spiritual power, as do the words of Dante, when, writing more than six centuries after the death of Gregory, he thus describes the potency of his prayers:

> " Fervent love
> And lively hope, with violence assail
> The kingdom of the heavens, and overcome
> The will of the Most High : not in such sort
> As man prevails o'er man ; but conquers it,
> Because 'tis willing to be conquer'd ; still,
> Though conquer'd, by its mercy, conquering."

The numerous pictures of St. Gregory as a single figure can usually be recognised from the dove, his peculiar symbol. He is frequently seen in the pontifical robes, with the tiara and crosier with the double cross ; all of which might be given to any Pope, but the dove, or a book, or an angel playing some musical instrument, indicate that Gregory the Great is the Pope represented.

St. Gregory is pictured in various scenes which illustrate his charity, gentleness, and other Christian virtues, but the three most impressive subjects connected with him are founded on legends, and are known as the Supper, the Mass of St. Gregory, and the Miracle of the Brandeum.

He was accustomed to have twelve poor men invited to his table, — in remembrance of the number of the Disciples, — and on one occasion he counted thirteen; he asked his steward why there were more than usual present, and although the man counted again and again he could see but twelve. When the supper was over, the Pope approached the stranger, asking "Who art thou?" and the man replied, "I am one whose necessities thou hast often relieved; my name is the Wonderful, and God will grant thy prayers, for my sake!"

In the Chapel of St. Barbara, in the Church of San Gregorio Magno, in Rome, there is a table, said to be that which the Pope used when he entertained the twelve poor men. A statue of St. Gregory is also here, and is said to have been begun by Michael Angelo, and finished by Cordieri. Two frescoes in this chapel represent the Supper, and the scene where the saint met the blond children in the Forum, whom he called angels, and who suggested to him the thought of sending missionaries to England.

In some pictures of the Supper, the stranger is represented as an angel, visible to the Pope alone. Veronese, in his fresco in Santa Maria del Monte, in Vicenza, makes him like Christ in the dress of a pilgrim, and Vasari, in his picture in the Bologna Gallery, also portrays the unknown like the Saviour. This picture is Vasari's masterpiece, and represents a scene of great legendary interest; it also contains portraits of men who were famous in Vasari's time, but the fact that the Pope in this picture is a likeness of Clement VII. makes the picture worthless as a representation of the Supper of St. Gregory; called by any other name, it would be more valuable.

The Mass of St. Gregory is not a pleasant picture. The legend runs that on an occasion when St. Gregory was officiating at the celebration of the Eucharist, some one doubted the real presence of Christ, and, in answer to the prayer of the saint, the crucified Saviour, with all the instruments of his suffering around him, appeared upon the altar. In the Church of San Gregorio this Vision of the Crucified is represented in the sculpture on the altar, in the chapel of the saint.

The legend of the Brandeum relates that

ANDREA SACCHI. — THE MIRACLE OF THE
BRANDEUM.

the Empress Constantia begged Gregory
to give her some portion of the relics of
SS. Peter and Paul, but he, not daring to
disturb the remains of these saints, sent
her a portion of the linen which had en-
veloped the remains of St. John the Evangelist.   Constantia rejected this gift with
scorn.   Then Gregory, desiring to prove
that the faith of the believer is the power
that works miracles, rather than the virtue
of any special relic, placed the cloth on
the altar, and, after praying, pierced it
with a knife, and blood flowed from it as
from a living body.

Over the altar of St. Gregory in St.
Peter's there is a mosaic copy of a picture of this miracle, after a painting by
Andrea Sacchi, which hangs in the Gallery of the Vatican.   Sacchi's pictures are
simple and direct in treatment, grave in
tone, and luminous in colour.   He was
not a great artist, but he imparted an

element of interest to his works, which secures them attention.

In this painting of the Brandeum, the altar is at the side of the picture, and the Pope, turning toward his attendants and the ambassadors of the empress, has pierced the linen, from which the blood flows. The astonishment of the witnesses is well portrayed; the dove hovers near the head of St. Gregory, and all the details of the work are well rendered.

There are few pictures of St. Gregory alone, or such as represent the incidents of his life, in European galleries, but in pictures of the Madonna, and of scenes from the life of Christ, he appears with the other Latin Fathers, as in the Enthroned Madonna in the Venetian Academy, of which I have spoken.

In funeral chapels the decorations frequently remind one that the doctrine of purgatory originated with St. Gregory,

who is represented as praying, while
angels release souls from the flames of
hell. He was believed to have thus released the soul of the Emperor Trajan
by prayer, and, as we have seen, Dante
attributed to his prayers the power to
"overcome the will of the Most High."

In Byzantine representations of the
Greek Fathers, or Doctors of the Church,
they are placed in much the same relation to Christ as are those of the Latin
Church. Having no distinguishing symbol, — each bearing a book or scroll, — the
name is necessarily inscribed near each
Father. The chief examples of this
representation are those of the dome
of the Baptistery of St. Mark, in Venice,
and of the Cathedral of Monreale, Pa-
lermo.

Saint John Chrysostom, the golden-
mouthed, is first among these Doctors,
and in the church in Venice which bears

his name there is a celebrated picture, in
which he is enthroned, and surrounded
by six saints, SS. Mary Magdalene, Catherine, Agnes, John the Baptist, Augustine, and Liberale. This is called the
masterpiece of Sebastian del Piombo,
who was not eminent in composition, and
lacked delicacy and spirituality. Even
here the female saints are conscious of
their personal attractions, and the male
saints also have a hint of affectation in
their bearing; this is especially true of
St. John the Baptist. In short, while
this is an effective picture, it lacks dignity and delicacy, and, while spirited, it is
imbued with impetuosity, rather than with
calm and commanding force.

In passing I must remark that in this
Church of San Giovanni Crisostomo is
the last picture signed by that genuinely
religious painter; Giovanni Bellini, when
he was eighty-four years old. It repre-

sents SS. Jerome, Christopher, and Augustine in a mountainous landscape.

I know of no pictures of St. Basil the Great, St. Athanasius, St. Gregory Nazianzen, and St. Cyril, sometimes named as a fifth Greek Doctor, that demand our consideration.

CHAPTER V.

PATRON SAINTS.

ATRON or protecting saints are of various orders, there being patrons of nations, cities, and towns; of orders, societies, schools, and hospitals; of physicians, soldiers, sailors, prisoners, travellers, invalids, and those who are weak; of students, philosophers, theologians, and other scholars; of young girls and women who teach; of women in childbirth; and of individuals in all professions and stations.

There are certain patron saints of both sexes, who have been venerated by all nations and in all periods since the Christian era. This is true of saints who have a Scriptural history, yet some of these have been adopted, and are considered as special patrons of certain localities, — as St. Peter at Rome, and St. Mark in Venice, — while, in another sense, they belong to all Christendom, and, as saints, must ever be accorded the highest honours. There are also saints who are greatly venerated as patrons in certain localities, who are rarely mentioned elsewhere; for example, SS. Justina and Rufina are most important in Seville, and almost unknown in Rome or Paris.

The universal patrons are represented in Art in the churches and religious and charitable edifices of all countries. We may lament, as we study these pictures and statues, that we are frequently reminded of the productions of pagan art, and that the simple stories of the New Testament are so supplemented with legends and traditions that these men of God are not recognisable by one who knows their Scripture story only; but we may comfort ourselves with the reflection that they represent aspects of the divine character of Christ, or some virtue to which we aspire. We may well believe that such beings as are thus represented were *Nothelper* — Helpers-in-need — in the ages of barbarity and violence, of ignorance and superstition, in which many of these conceptions originated.

Among these universal patrons the first place is accorded to *St. George of England*, the hero of the " Faerie Queene." He is also the patron of Germany, and shares the honours of Venice with St. Mark, while he is the protector of soldiers and armourers, wherever saints are venerated.

As St. Michael overcame Satan himself, as Apollo and Perseus destroyed the monsters of mythology, so St. George

slew the evil one, under the usual form
of a dragon, who ravaged the flocks and
herds, and even destroyed the children of
a certain city in Libya. So much feared
was this monster that, at length, two children, drawn by lot, were daily given him
to appease his wrath, and a day arrived
when the lovely daughter of the king was
the victim to be sacrificed.

As the maiden was going forth to meet
her fate, St. George appeared, and making
the sign of the cross, and calling on Christ
for strength, he overcame the dragon after
a terrible conflict, and the beast having
been bound with the girdle of the princess, she led him, perfectly subdued, within
the walls of the city. As a result of this
prowess of the saint, twenty thousand
people embraced the faith of which they
had witnessed the power, and were baptised in one day.

I will not recount all the sufferings to

which St. George was subjected by the Emperor Dacian, before he was finally beheaded, which persecutions gained for him the title of the Great Martyr, in the Greek Church.

To the Crusaders St. George was the ideal military saint, and in 1222 his feast was made a holiday. A century later, in 1330, the institution of the Order of the Garter confirmed his title as chief patron of England, where there are one hundred and sixty-two churches dedicated to him.

Devotional pictures of St. George are numerous, and embrace single figures of the saint, or representations of his combat with the dragon, or Madonna pictures in which he is introduced. Of single figures I will mention but one, the statue by Donatello, on the exterior of Or San Michele, Florence. It is the personification of dignified nobility and serious, calm determination, such as one would

desire in a defender, in peace or in war.
He leans on his shield, on which the
cross is seen; his head is bare, and his
person protected by a complete suit of
armour. One would scarcely look for
the same conception of this saint by
Donatello and Spenser, but the sculptor's
statue and the poet's lines are in accord.

"Upon his shield the bloodie cross was scored,
  For sovereign help, which in his need he had.
  Right faithful, true he was, in deed and word;
  But of his cheere did seem too solemn sad;
  Yet nothing did he dread, but ever was ydrad."

In Gothic sculpture and in French art
St. George appears but rarely, and is then
in company with other military saints.

In pictures of St. George and the
Dragon there may be a certain resemblance to those of St. Michael, but there
are also such differences as make it easy
to distinguish each from the other. St.

Michael has wings, and a balance; St. George has the martyr's palm; St. Theodore, too, appears with a dragon, but that on which he stands in the Piazzetta, at Venice, can only be called a dragon by courtesy; it is a crocodile, and, in any case, it seems unlikely that St. George and the Dragon can be mistaken for any other subject.

Tintoretto, Rubens, Raphael, Ludovico Caracci, and Lucas von. Leyden all painted their conceptions of the struggle between the saint and the monster. Albert Dürer made four different prints representing it. Schwanthaler embodied his idea of it in a fine bas-relief, and it has been many times pictured by lesser artists.

The two small pictures by Raphael, in the galleries of the Louvre and the Hermitage, differ much in spirit. The first, called St. George with the Sword, represents the mail-clad saint on a white horse,

at the moment when he is about to strike
off the dragon's head; the monster, with
open mouth and uplifted claw, is too near
the leg of the saint for safety. The landscape background is desolate, with two
stunted trees; in the distance the princess
is escaping. The figure of the saint is
elegant, and his face that of a happy youth,
perfectly certain of victory over his revolting foe.

The St. Petersburg picture is the St.
George of the Garter. Henry VII. had
sent the Order and Insignia of the Garter
to Duke Guidobaldo, and Count Castigli-
one was sent to England to be knighted
as proxy for the duke, and, with other
gifts, he carried this St. George to Henry.
After many changes it now hangs beside
the great portrait of the Emperor Alexander, having a burning lamp continually
before it. Here, too, the saint is on a
white horse, and, rushing forward, has

transfixed the dragon with his lance, while the princess, in the background, is kneeling in prayer. Under his right knee the saint wears the Order of St. George, or the Garter.

Tintoretto also painted this subject twice, one picture being in the Ducal Palace, Venice, and the other in the National Gallery. That in Venice differs much from other pictures of the subject. The princess is astride the dragon's neck, he being bridled with a ribbon which the maiden holds. St. George, standing behind, holds his hands above her head, either to bless the princess, or by a miraculous power to quiet the dragon. A monk is near, watching the group. The princess is richly dressed; the face of the saint is beautiful; his gray armour and drapery are in clear relief against the sky. Of this work, Ruskin says: " There is no expression or life in the dragon, though

ERCOLE GRANDI. — ST. GEORGE.

the white flashes in the eye are very
ghastly: but the whole thing is entirely
typical; and the princess is not so much
represented as riding the dragon, as supposed to be placed by St. George in an
attitude of perfect victory over her chief
enemy." Here, as in all other representations of this and kindred subjects, we
understand that their real intent is to
symbolise the conquest of evil by good.

The picture by Rubens, in the Queen's
Gallery, was painted for Charles I., the
saint and princess being portraits of the
king and his queen. The Thames and
Windsor Castle are seen in the distance.
Here, St. George, with his foot on the
dragon, gives the princess the end of
the girdle that she may lead the conquered
monster. Two groups of spectators observe the scene, while angels descend from
above with a crown and laurel for the
victor.

A quaint picture is that by Ercole Grandi, in the Corsini Gallery, Rome. It explains itself with great frankness. The dragon is pinned to the earth by the weapon which transfixes his body, and when the saint's sword descends, the prayer of the princess will doubtless be answered.

In the Church of San Giorgio degli Schiavoni, Venice, are pictures of St. George and the Dragon, the Reception of the Saint by the Father of the Princess and the Conversion and Baptism of the King and his Court. These are by Carpaccio, whom Kugler calls "the historical painter of the elder Venetian School." He certainly represented the daily life of Venice in a masterly manner, no matter what subject he painted. His backgrounds are rich with landscape, imposing edifices, and other accessories, and his colouring is deep and powerful.

Veronese, Rubens, and Vandyck all

painted the Martyrdom of St. George, and it is needless to say that they are all fine works of art. The first two follow the legend that the saint was beheaded, but Vandyck pictures his being sacrificed to an idol. The work of Veronese is in the Church of San Giorgio, Verona; that of Rubens in the Church of San Giorgio de Lière, near Antwerp, and that by Vandyck in a private collection.

I know of no Madonna picture in which St. George appears that is so attractive as that by Correggio, in the Dresden Gallery. The Virgin is enthroned in the midst of open architecture, and the whole scene is flooded with brilliant daylight. SS. Peter, John Baptist, and Geminianus are also represented. Boy angels play with the armour of St. George, in the foreground. The picture has all the grace and sweetness of Correggio's best manner, and belongs to the period of his greatest power.

When we consider *St. Sebastian*, the universal protector against plague and pestilence, we find more historical fact connected with his life than is the case with many other saints. He came of a noble family in Gaul, was a commander in the Prætorian Guards, and a favourite with the Emperor Diocletian. Being secretly a Christian, the practice of Christian virtues rendered him singularly attractive to his associates, while his position enabled him to protect other Christians from persecution. At length, however, two young Christian soldiers were condemned to death, — after firmly enduring torture, — and the prayers of their families had almost persuaded them to recant, when Sebastian, careless of his own safety, eloquently encouraged them to meet death rather than deny Christ. So enthusiastically did he picture the Christian life, here and hereafter, that those who heard him were converted and baptised, including the judge himself. ,

This boldness sealed Sebastian's fate. Diocletian reasoned with him, endeavouring to save his life, — for he loved his faithful young guardsman, — but failing in his efforts, he condemned Sebastian to be bound, and shot to death with arrows. This being done, the saint was left for dead, but his friends who came to bury him discovered that he still lived, and secretly nursed him back to health.

After his recovery, the Christians urged him to fly from Rome, but Sebastian placed himself in the path of the emperor, as he left the palace, and when Diocletian appeared Sebastian entreated him to spare the lives of the Christians who had been condemned to death. Diocletian exclaimed, " Art thou not Sebastian ? " and when the truth was told him, he commanded that Sebastian should be beaten to death with clubs, and his body thrown into the Cloaca Maxima. The Christians, however, rescued the corpse, and buried it in the catacombs, at the feet of SS. Peter and Paul.

The shooting with arrows doubtless caused Sebastian to be chosen as a protector against pestilence. He did not, like some other saints, devote himself to the care of the plague-stricken, but arrows, from the most ancient days, have been the symbol of pestilence. In regions subject to such diseases there are many churches dedicated to St. Sebastian.

Pictures of this saint, almost without exception, represent his martyrdom. Even when he is introduced in various religious subjects, with other saints, one or more arrows were customarily used to emphasise his personality. He is pictured as young, semi-nude, and bound to a tree or column; he is of a noble figure and fine

GUIDO RENI. — ST. SEBASTIAN.

countenance, and gazes heavenward with an expression of spiritual ecstasy; angels frequently are seen descending with the martyr's crown and palm, and in some cases his armour is introduced as an emblem of his military profession.

There is little variety in the manner of representing St. Sebastian, and this little is seen in the backgrounds and in minor details, but there is a great difference in the effect of the pictures. The earliest examples are stiff, badly modelled, and sometimes absurd in their unnatural posing and their curious details. Later St. Sebastian became a favourite subject with artists, affording as it did a fine opportunity for anatomical modelling and the representation of Apollo-like beauty. Almost numberless pictures were thus produced which are recognised at a glance.

Guido Reni's picture in the Capitoline Museum, Rome, is an excellent example of these works, which display the skill of this artist, who painted this subject seven or eight times.

In the Scuola di San Rocco, Venice, there is a St. Sebastian by Tintoretto, which Ruskin calls "the most majestic St. Sebastian in existence, as far as mere humanity can be majestic, for there is no effort at any expression of angelic or saintly resignation : the effort is simply to realise the fact of the martyrdom, and it seems to me that this is done to an extent not even attempted by any other painter. . . . The face, in spite of its ghastliness, is beautiful, and has been serene ; and the light which enters first and glistens on the plumes of the arrows dies softly away upon the curling hair and mixes with the glory upon the forehead. There is not a more remarkable picture in Venice."

Unfortunately this picture is on a space between the windows and has as bad a light as possible. By shading the eyes it can be seen comparatively well at some hours of the day, and one should visit this wonderful Scuola many times.

Of the few pictures illustrating the life of St. Sebastian, those by Veronese, in the Church of San Sebastiano, Venice, merit the first mention. The finest of these represents the saint on the way to his martyrdom. He descends a flight of steps, dressed in full armour and waving a banner, while exhorting the two young Christians not to deny their faith. It is a picture to arouse enthusiasm, and few can study it without feeling a deep sympathy with the young Christian orator, who is thus courting death for the sake of the faith which was in him. The picture is aglow with light, and the variety of persons in the groups of spectators afforded Veronese the opportunity to represent many types of character, which he so well knew how to improve. It is a work of immense dramatic power, and some good critics prefer this before all other pictures by Veronese. Kugler considers it the noblest work of the great Venetian, in some respects. Indeed, the skill and beauty of its composition, the richness of the sentiment so powerfully expressed, the life and excitement of the scene, combined with its glorious colour, make this a masterpiece in painting. The pictures of Veronese in the Church of San Sebastiano, where the walls and altars are rich with his works, may be regarded as a glorious monument to himself, since he is buried here, and they well serve to perpetuate his fame, while they honour St. Sebastian.

There are several interesting statues of St. Sebastian; that in the church dedicated to the saint, in the environs of Rome, which was designed by Bernini, is esteemed as the finest conception of this sculptor; it was executed by Giorgini, who lovingly interpreted the intention of his master.

In the Cathedral of Lucca, in a small octagonal chapel of marble, erected in 1484, in which is kept the sacred crucifix, shown but three times a year, there is a statue of St. Sebastian, dating from 1470, that is famous as the first undraped statue produced in Italy, after the Renaissance in Art. The saint is represented bound to a tree and pierced with several gilt arrows; the pose of the figure and the expression of the face are admirable and redeem the work from its other defects. The chapel and the statue are the work of Matteo Civitale.

In the Church of Santa Maria, in Carignano, Genoa, is a colossal statue of St. Sebastian by Puget, a follower of Bernini. Here also the saint is transfixed, and his armour is at his feet; it is an effective, pretentious work.

In our day it seems quite unnecessary that protectors against the plague should be especially venerated in Western Christendom, but during the Middle Ages this scourge frequently visited all seaports that were in commercial communication with the Orient. This was especially true of ports on the eastern coast of Italy; terrible visitations of the plague devastated Southern Europe, and even swept over London with terrific results. These considerations explain the need that was felt for more than one protecting saint against these dreaded evils. After St. Sebastian, the most important of these is *St. Roch*, who is seen in many religious pictures. Much of the interest in this saint is centred in the Church and Scuola di San Rocco, Venice.

The church was built to receive the relics of the saint, which had been stolen from Montpelier, the home of the saint,

G. CHIARI. — MARY MAGDALENE.

and carried to Venice, where the visitations of the plague were frequent. The
church was built by a community of men
who cared for the sick and suffering, many
of its members belonging to noble and
wealthy families. The Scuola di San
Rocco, so magnificently decorated by Tintoretto and his pupils, was connected with
the church, and contained the council-halls
of the community.

The principal facts in the life of St.
Roch are well authenticated, and he is
thought to be entitled to special reverence
on account of his having contracted the
plague in caring for the sick. He suffered
all its horrors in a secret place to which
he dragged himself, in order that he should
not expose others to its dangers, and his
only attendant was a little dog, who
brought food to his master. When recov-
ering, St. Roch dragged himself to Montpelier, where he was not recognised, and

was arrested as a spy and sent to prison by his own uncle, who did not know his nephew in the wasted prisoner. In prison he died; his dungeon was filled with supernatural light, and beside his body was a writing disclosing his identity and promising that the plague-stricken who prayed to St. Roch should be healed.

Devotional pictures represent him as a pilgrim with staff, cloak, wallet, and cockleshell. His little dog is frequently with him, and the saint usually lifts his robe to disclose a plague spot. A small picture by Garofalo, in the Belvedere, Vienna, is a good example of these representations, in which the subject is easily recognised. In the Scuola di San Rocco, decorated by Tintoretto, one picture represents the saint in the presence of God; it is on the centre of the ceiling. Of this Ruskin says: "It is quite different from his common work; bright in all its tints and tones; the faces carefully drawn, and of an agreeable type; the outlines firm, and the shadows few; the whole resembling Correggio." In this remarkable Scuola there are fifty-seven pictures by Tintoretto. Here is also a statue of St. Roch by Campagna, in the lower hall, while in the upper hall there are scenes from the life of the saint in bas-reliefs, on panels of oak, by Marchiori.

In the Church of San Rocco are five scenes from the life of St. Roch, also by Tintoretto. They are St. Roch in the Wilderness, St. Roch in the Hospital, St. Roch Healing Animals, The Capture of St. Roch, and an Angel appearing to the Saint in Prison.

One cannot approve of all the works of Tintoretto, and Kugler's estimate of him, which follows, expresses the truth in a few words; while one finds great pleasure in the study of his numerous and vast

canvases, there is still something to be
desired. " His off-hand style, as we may
call it, is, it is true, always full of grand
and meaning detail; with a few patches of
colour he expresses sometimes the liveliest
forms and expressions; but he fails in
that artistic arrangement of the whole,
and in that nobility of motives in parts,
which are necessary exponents of a high
idea. His compositions are not expressed
by finely studied degrees of participation
in the principal action, but by great masses
of light and shade. . . . With Titian the
highest idea of earthly happiness in existence is expressed by beauty; with Tintoretto in mere animal strength, sometimes
of a very rude character."

Rubens painted for the Confraternity of
St. Roch, at Alost, a large altar-piece, on
which he spent but a week; it so pleased
the monks that they paid him eight hundred florins, after which the artist gave

them three smaller works, which were placed beneath the larger one. The upper portion of the large picture represents St. Roch in his prison, ablaze with heavenly light, kneeling to receive from Christ his mission as a protector against the plague. In the lower part is a group of the afflicted, praying the saint for his aid. The whole is painted with the great power of the famous Belgian master.

Votive pictures are frequently seen in hospitals, churches, and chapels dedicated to St. Roch, in which he is represented as having healed the donor.

Akin to the offices of SS. Sebastian and Roch were those of the brothers, *SS. Cosmo* and *Damian*, known as the saintly Arab physicians. They were patrons of medicine and physicians, and of the Medici family. Having studied their profession for the sake of caring for the suffering, they came to be the most skilful physicians that had been known before, or in their time. In the reign of Diocletian they were beheaded.

In the Greek Church, the devotions that had been paid to Esculapius were transferred to these saints, and in the sixth century Pope Felix IV. erected a church in their honour in the Forum. The Greek mosaics in this church are doubtless the most ancient existing representations of these holy brothers.

In devotional pictures SS. Cosmo and Damian appear in the conventional garb of a physician, "in scarlet gown, furred well." Their symbols are a pestle and mortar, ointment boxes, or a lancet. A picture by Titian, commemorating the plague in Venice in 1512, now in Santa Maria della Salute, interested me more than any representation of these saints that I have seen. They are with St. Mark, the chief patron of Venice, and

Ruskin says: "The small Titian, St. Mark with SS. Cosmo and Damian, was, when I first saw it, to my judgment, by far the first work of Titian's in Venice."

Pictures illustrative of the lives and legends of these saints are rare, and I know of none that are important.

While *St. Christopher* is not the patron of any one class of people, he is the giant saint, whose story is intended to encourage all who are in need to realise that divine aid is ever near. The sight of him is believed to strengthen the weak and weary; a Latin inscription, when translated, runs, "Whoever shall behold the image of St. Christopher shall not faint or fail on that day!"

His beautiful legend relates that Offero sought the most powerful sovereign in the world, that he might serve him, and finding that even sovereigns feared Satan, Offero served him, and finding that Satan feared Christ, he sought his service, and was greatly afflicted at not finding him.

At length, as Offero slept in his hut beside a river, where he was accustomed to aid those who wished to cross the stream, he heard the voice of a child begging to be carried to the opposite bank. To this Offero gladly consented, and raising the child to his shoulder, and taking his strong staff, he entered the water. The child, who was easily enough carried at the start, grew heavy and heavier, until, in the middle of the stream, Offero feared that both he and the child would be drowned. Then he exclaimed, "Who art thou? had I borne the whole world it could not have been heavier!" And the child replied: "Thou hast borne not only the world but the maker of it on thy shoulders; henceforth thou shalt serve me. Plant thy staff and it shall put forth leaves and fruit."

FIORENZO DI LORENZO — ST. CHRISTOPHER.

Then Offero became a Christian and his name was changed to Christopher, — the bearer of Christ, — and he went about doing good until the time of his martyrdom in Samos. He is easily recognised in works of art by his size and his enormous staff, which is never omitted.

Scenes from the life of St. Christopher are rare. The Church of Santa Maria dell Orto, Venice, is also called the Church of St. Christopher, the Martyr, and there is Tintoretto's picture of his martyrdom, which is a good example of the manner of this master, already mentioned.

In the Church of the Eremitani, Padua, a chapel dedicated to SS. James and Christopher is important in the history of Art in Northern Italy, and it is still imposing in effect in spite of what it has suffered by decay and restorations. The picture of St. Christopher bearing the

child is by a poor artist, Bono, of Ferrara.
The pictures of the Martyrdom of the
Saint and the Removal of his Body are
interesting examples of the work of that
very important fifteenth century master,
Andrea Mantegna. A son-in-law of Jacopo
Bellini, his style was doubtless influenced
by him, and some writers and art critics
attribute to Mantegna a great influence
on the most famous artists of the Venetian school. In the " History of Painting
in North Italy," Crowe and Cavalcaselle,
we read :

" Here it is that we become fully acquainted with Mantegna's lofty position
among artists. Here we mark how much
more gifted he was in some senses than
the celebrated men of the following century. We compare his giant figure with
Titian's David and Goliath, or the Death
of Abel in the ceiling of the sacristy of
the Salute in Venice, and we perceive

that the great Venetian lives on the achievements of the Paduan, content to enjoy the fruit garnered by Mantegna, who for his part fixes rules indispensable to the future expansion of Art. . . . It was necessary that some one should be found, to level the road leading to perfection; and such an one we justly recognise in Mantegna, who, without sense of spontaneous or ideal grace, and without feeling for colour, had the power and indomitable will of Donatello and Buonarotti."

St. Nicholas of Myra is important, since he is the patron saint of Russia, Bari, Venice, Freiburg, and many other towns and cities. He is also the protector of children, especially of schoolboys, of travellers, merchants, sailors, and poor maidens, as well as a guardain saint against thieves and violence, or losses by robbers. He is best known to us as *Santa Claus*, and all over Christendom he is known as the saint of the people, especially of the poor, and has no rival in the affection of the young. In A. D. 560, the Emperor Justinian dedicated a church to St. Nicholas, in Constantinople, and since then, in Europe and in Great Britain, where there are three hundred and seventy-six, a greater number of churches and chapels have been dedicated to St. Nicholas than to any other saint.

The facts in relation to this saint seem to resolve themselves into the statement that from infancy he was religious and entered the priesthood; he devoted his life to good works, and died peacefully in Myra, and was buried in a splendid church.

After his death great miracles were performed at his tomb, and many cities desired possession of his remains. In Bari it is claimed that the bones of the saint were brought there in 1084, and a magnificent church was erected as his tomb. The Venetians make the same claim, but by general consent he is called St. Nicholas of Bari. The story of his miracles and remarkable experiences would fill a small volume; many of these have been illustrated in Art.

Being the most popular saint of the Greek Church, he is more frequently seen in the devotional pictures of that church than is any other saint. In these he wears the dress of a bishop, with neither mitre or crosier, bearing the cross alone, while the three Persons of the Trinity are embroidered on his cope.

In the devotional pictures of the Western Church St. Nicholas is represented in bishop's robes, with mitre, crosier, jewelled gloves, and a magnificently embroidered cope. A fine picture of this description, by Botticelli, is in the Capitoline Museum, Rome. His attribute is three balls, to

which various meanings are ascribed.
The most frequent explanation is that
they signify three purses that the saint
gave to save the daughters of a poor man
from a dishonourable life; again, they
stand for loaves of bread which he distributed to the hungry; while others see in
them a symbol of the Trinity. If sitting,
the balls are in his lap; if standing, they
are at his feet, or he carries a book on
which the balls are placed. Rarely these
balls are replaced by three purses, and
again, by three children, referring to a
miracle by which he restored to life three
children who had been murdered. An
anchor, or a ship in the distance, refers
to St. Nicholas as the patron of seamen.

A beautiful picture of St. Nicholas is
in the so-called Anseidei Madonna, by
Raphael, at Blenheim. The Virgin and
child are reading a book; St. Nicholas,
on one side, is reading the Scriptures;

his face is singularly sweet and benevolent.

The visit by night which St. Nicholas
paid to the house of the poor man, when
he threw the purses containing the dow-
ries for the daughters in at the window,
has been more frequently represented than
has any other incident of his legend. The
quaint picture of this scene, by Fra Angelico, is in the Vatican. Through the
open doorway of the house, the poor father
is seen, sitting in the corridor, in a de-
jected attitude; in a room beyond the
three maidens, asleep in bed, are visible.
At one side the saint is throwing the
purses in through an open window. The
story is most simply told, the work, though
in colours, being scarcely more than outline.

CHAPTER VI.

THE VIRGIN PATRONESSES AND THE GREAT VIRGINS OF THE LATIN CHURCH.

F the Four Virgin Patronesses Mrs. Jameson says: "We owe to these beautiful and glorious impersonations of feminine intellect, heroism, purity, fortitude, and faith, some of the most excelling works of art which have been handed down to us. Other female martyrs were merely women glorified in heaven, for virtues exercised on earth; but *these* were absolutely, in all but the name, Divinities."

In the study of Art one learns to ·be grateful to these saints, whose lives, and the traditions concerning them, exercised such an influence on the minds of artists as stimulated them to the production of some of the most glorious works in existence.

To the scholarly and thoughtful Christians in the blossoming time of religious art, the legends of these saints appealed on the æsthetic and poetic side, while to the unlearned they were to be relied on with absolutely unfailing faith. The Almighty might not hear and answer prayers that were breathed on earth, but if one of these holy virgins would present such petitions at his throne, all would be well. To these believing, trusting souls, beautiful pictures of these virgin saints were like heavenly visions.

We cannot accept these legends in the mediæval spirit, as they were accepted by the artists who painted, and the devout who gazed in rapture on their works, but we can accept them as figurative and reverently discern their allegorical meaning; and in so doing we shall find a pleasure in religious art that can be attained in no other way.

St. Catherine of Alexandria was unknown in the Western Church until the Crusaders, who believed that she had aided them in the East, introduced her name, life, and legends to European countries, in which she was soon devoutly venerated. She is patroness of learning, of students of all grades and classes, of educational institutions, and of eloquence. Of Venice she is a protector, and a favourite saint with ladies of noble birth, she having been of royal blood.

Her legend and even her existence have been doubted, but she retains her place in Art undisturbed, and in the hearts of saint-loving people she ranks next to Mary Magdalene. Even in England more than fifty churches are dedicated to her.

CARLO DOLCI. — ST. CATHERINE OF ALEXANDRIA.

To men she is a patroness of learning; to women, an ever present example of wisdom and purity.

Devotional pictures of St. Catherine represent her alone, as venerable, or grouped with other saints in Madonna and other pictures. As a patroness she has several symbols in common with other saints, as the book, indicating her learning; the palm of a martyr; the crown of a princess; and the sword, by which she died; but her distinctive attribute, which is rarely omitted, is the wheel by which the emperor desired to torture her; when the wheel is broken the miracle by which she was saved is symbolised. It is placed by her side, or at her feet, and in some cases is borne aloft by angels.

The legend relates that two wheels in which knives were inserted were prepared, and Catherine was to be placed between them, and cut into a thousand bits by their revolutions. But when the saint was bound to these wheels an angel appeared, and fire from heaven burned the wheels and the fragments were scattered.

Catherine is represented in the dress of a princess, and usually wears a diadem. She is dignified and refined in person, with an intellectual and earnest countenance. Her representations are very numerous, having been executed in various kinds of engraving, as well as on canvas and in frescoes, and are readily recognised by the wheel, which is rarely omitted.

The beautiful small picture by Raphael, in the National Gallery, is praised by universal consent. It represents the saint to the knees; her right arm is folded on her breast, while the left rests on the wheel. She gazes at a bright spot in the sky with an expression of joyous peace. The background is a lovely landscape. One can but agree with Passavant, when he says:

"It is one of those works which nothing can describe; neither words, nor a painted copy, nor engravings, for the fire in it appears living, and is entirely beyond imitation."

The picture in the Belvedere, Vienna, by Palma Vecchio, in which the St. Catherine is said to be a portrait of the beautiful Violante, daughter of the artist, is a pleasing Madonna picture. Catherine is kneeling at the feet of the Virgin, in a rich Venetian costume, and wearing her crown as a princess. Whenever this saint is represented as a patroness of Venice by Venetian masters, she appears as a beautiful, regal woman, rather than as a learned or religious one. Several of these pictures are portraits, notably that by Titian, which is a likeness of Caterina Cornaro; Veronese and Tintoretto also painted figures of St. Catherine which impress us as portraits. A Madonna and Child, by Titian, and a Holy Family, by Veronese, in both of which St. Catherine is represented, are in the Uffizi.

As a patroness of learning St. Catherine is frequently in the company of St. Jerome and other Doctors of the Church; as patroness of Venice she is associated with St. George; in other pictures her frequent companions are SS. Barbara and Mary Magdalene.

Titian painted a magnificent altar-piece for the Frari, Venice, which is now in the gallery of the Vatican. It represents St. Nicholas gazing upward, as one inspired; St. Peter looks over the shoulder of the first named saint at a book, and a lovely St. Catherine stands on the other side of St. Nicholas; in the background are SS. Francis, Antony of Padua, and Sebastian. In the clouds the Madonna and child are seen, the latter holding a wreath, as if to crown a saint, while two attending infant

angels also have wreaths in their hands;
it is a glorious picture. Painted in Titian's
later manner, it is an excellent example
of the so-called *Santa Conversazione*,
which pictures were less restrained in
their composition than when the Madonna
was enthroned in the centre; in these
works the throne may be at the side, or in
the background, or omitted entirely.

In the Vatican there is also a St. Catherine, by Murillo, which Taine describes
as "of a strange, disturbing attractive-
ness. Her beauty is of a dangerous order;
her oblique glance and black downcast
eyes gleam with a secret ardour. . . . In
Raphael's works, the repose which sober
colour gives and a sculptural attitude de-
prive the eyes of a portion of their vivacity.
Spanish colour, on the contrary, is quiv-
ering; the unconscious sensuality of an
ardent nature, the sudden palpitation of
fugitive vehement emotions, the nervous

excitement of voluptuousness and ecstasy, the force, the rage, of internal fires, lurk in that flesh illuminated by its own intensity, in those ruddy tints drowned in those deep, mysterious darks."

The Marriage of St. Catherine is a lovely picture, whatever may be the light in which it is viewed.   To the Church it is a devotional subject; its mystical teaching is that of the close spiritual bond between Christ and his followers.   When the Madonna, Child, and saint only are represented the subject assumes its most serious and dignified aspect, but angels, flowers, and other beautiful symbols are in harmony with its picturesque and poetic elements.   When saints and other sacred personages are introduced as witnesses, increasing the dramatic interest, the whole is still concordant, and the mystical and deeply devotional character of the scene is not lessened.

The legend which this picture illustrates relates that, being the heiress to a kingdom, it was important that Catherine should marry, which she was constantly urged to do. But no suitor could be suggested whom she would accept. It happened that an old hermit gave Catherine a picture of the Virgin and Child, and from that time she could think of Jesus alone, and loved him with all her soul.

In a dream she went with the hermit to a sanctuary on a high mountain, where she was met by a company of angels, and fell on her face before them; but one of these heavenly messengers called her to follow him, and leading Catherine before the Queen of Heaven, the angel begged her to accept the maiden as a daughter. The Virgin then presented Catherine to her Son, who, regarding her, said, "She is not fair enough for me." Then Catherine awoke, and, seeking the hermit, inquired what she must do to be worthy of this celestial bridegroom.

When the hermit had instructed Catherine and her mother in the true faith, they were baptised, and in a second dream the Virgin appeared, attended by many angels, and, again leading the maiden to Jesus, said: "Lo, she hath been baptised, and I am her godmother." Then Jesus smiled on Catherine, and pledged his troth to her, and placed a ring on her finger. When the maiden awoke the ring was there, and from that time she desired no earthly blessing, but longed to go to her Heavenly Bridegroom.

When the Emperor Maximin persecuted the Christians of Alexandria, Catherine was one of his victims. After many sufferings she was beheaded, and angels bore her body to Mount Sinai and placed it in a marble sarcophagus, above which, in the eighth century, a monastery was built. The picture of Angels Bearing her Remains through the air, by Mücke, is as beautiful as it is familiar, by means of the reproductions of it.

Of the pictures of the Marriage of St. Catherine much might be written, as many artists have painted this subject, in a great variety of methods. Many persons prefer before all others the picture by Titian, now in the Pitti, in which the Child Jesus is seated on a pedestal, and supported by the Virgin; St. Catherine kneels before him, and St. Anna holds her hand while the ring is placed on her finger. In the background are two angels, and St. Joseph stands at one side.

This composition is much more simple and sincere than are those of other Venetian artists who lavished their wonderful powers of imaginative detail upon this subject, and introduced a variety of luxurious features; for example, making the scene of this mystical marriage a gorgeous palace, suitable for the banquets which they so magnificently portrayed, but quite out of keeping with this motive.

Correggio painted this subject twice; the smaller picture, in the Museum at Naples, is rarely mentioned, the larger one, in the Louvre, being better known and far more important. This has been intensely admired by art lovers and critics. It is the picture of which Vasari said that such heads could be painted in Paradise only. Correggio's saint bends down in great humility, while in Titian's picture she bows the head alone; here the Virgin herself unites the hands of the Saviour and the saint; St. Sebastian stands at one side holding his arrows, while in the background the martyrdoms of the two saints are represented. To such subjects Correggio imparted an atmosphere of

MURILLO. — THE MARRIAGE OF ST. CATHERINE.

pious rapture, which is very noticeable in this work.

In the Church of the Augustines, in Antwerp, is Rubens's picture of this mystical marriage, which is occurring in the midst of such an assemblage of saints that it has the air of a social function, to which guests have been invited. It is a magnificent picture, but the mysticism, poetry, and grace of the legend are lost, — they find no place in such a representation.

Taken for all in all, I have seen no Marriage of St. Catherine which so strongly appeals to me as that by Murillo, which was presented to Pope Pius IX. by the Queen of Spain; it is in the gallery of the Vatican. In considering it I recall the quotation from Taine, already given, and agree with Viardot when he says that " Murillo comes up, in every respect, to what our imagination could hope or con-

ceive. . . . We find in the attitude of the
saints, and the expression of their features, all that the most ardent piety, all
that the most passionate exaltation, can
feel or express in extreme surprise, delight, and adoration." In contrasting
Velasquez and Murillo, Viardot calls the
former "the painter of the earth, and
Murillo of heaven."

St. Barbara is a very different type of
saint from St. Catherine; she may fitly
be called a Christian Minerva or Pallas
Athena. The protector of armourers, gun-
smiths, and fortifications, she is invoked
against accidents from explosions, and
from thunder and lightning. Her beauty
was so great that her father, fearing that
she would be sought in marriage, kept
her imprisoned in a high tower. Here
she reflected and studied, until she rejected the idols of her people, and entered
into a correspondence with Origen, who

sent to her a Christian teacher, in the guise of a physician, by whom she was converted.

When her father discovered this he denounced Barbara to the proconsul, and when all possible methods to induce her to recant had been tried in vain, her father took her to a high mountain and decapitated her with his own sword. While descending the mountain, a frightful tempest, with thunder and lightning, fell on him, and he was seen no more.

In devotional pictures, the sword, palm, and book are given to St. Barbara, but her distinctive symbol is the tower, which, if small, she holds when standing, and rests on her lap if sitting; or it may be a massive structure in the background. A belief existed in the early Church that those who chose St. Barbara as a patron saint could not die impenitent, from which it resulted that a sacramental cup

and wafer were added to her other symbols, in works of art.

Other pictures of St. Barbara are unimportant when compared with that by
Palma Vecchio, in Santa Maria Formosa,
Venice. It is said that this St. Barbara,
like the St. Catherine already mentioned,
and the Flora, by Titian, in the Uffizi,
are all portraits of Palma's daughter
Violante, famous not only for her beauty,
but as having been the first love of the
great artist, who represented her as the
Roman goddess of spring and flowers.

In the St. Barbara we see a majestic
woman, with eyes raised to heaven. Her
golden hair is crowned by a diadem, and
a white veil is gracefully disposed about
the head without concealing its beauty.
Her robe is of a deep, rich brown, her
mantle is crimson. There is an unusual
feeling of harmony in this work; the
beauty of the saint, the glow of colour,

PALMA VECCHIO. -- ST. BARBARA.

the healthful force and life of the impressive figure are, so to speak, fused one into another, producing a whole of which Taine says: "She is no saint, but a blooming young girl, the most attractive and lovable that one can imagine. . . . Two streams of magnificent brown hair glide down on either side of her neck; her delicate hands seem to be those of a goddess; her beautiful eyes are beaming, and her fresh and delicate lips are about to smile; she displays the gay and noble spirit of Venetian women; ample and not too full, *spirituelle* and benevolent, she seems to be made to give happiness to herself and others."

In this picture St. Barbara's tower is in the background, and the cannon are at her feet.

SS. Catherine and Barbara are frequent companions in works of art, and symbolise the active and the contemplative life;

they appear thus in German pictures, in which St. Barbara sometimes has a feather in her hand, referring to a German version of her legend which relates that, when her father scourged her, angels changed the scourge to feathers. This is seen in an exquisitely finished and beautiful Madonna picture in which St. Barbara appears, by Hugo van der Goes, now in the Uffizi.

The most famous picture in which St. Barbara is associated with the Virgin Mary is that in the Dresden Gallery, by Raphael, in which she is kneeling opposite to St. Sixtus, from whom it is called the Madonna di San Sisto. Her tower in the background is partly concealed by the curtain at the side of the picture. This famous work, as a whole, is a lofty expression of Christian poetry in painting. Passavant says of it that the saints are praying to the Virgin in behalf of the faithful; St. Sixtus is pointing toward them, and St. Barbara, with hands folded on her breast, and eyes cast down, has an admirable expression of sweetness and charity. She is a very different being from the saint of Palma Vecchio's great work. In studying this immortal painting, when one can turn from the Madonna and child, the St. Barbara is a delight.

As a protectress against sudden death, and a patroness of firearms, effigies of St. Barbara were frequently seen on shields and other armour, as well as on large field-pieces. In the Tower of London a suit of armour which belonged to Henry VIII. is ornamented with comparative scenes from the lives of St. Barbara and St. George; for example, St. George is accused before the emperor and St. Barbara is pursued by her father; St. George is tortured and St. Barbara is scourged, and thus the two lives are paralleled. The

designs are well engraved and one is fully
repaid for his trouble in examining this
fifteenth century German style of orna-
mentation for arms and armour.

Those who are acquainted with the
usual method of representing *St. Ursula*,
in which, under the voluminous folds of
her cloak, she shelters great numbers of
pigmy maidens, will understand that she
is the patroness of young girls, especially
of those still in school, and of all women
who educate and care for young maidens.

There can be no more extravagant and
improbable legend than that of St. Ursula.
Volumes have been written in arguing for
and against its verity; it has been explained as a delightful allegory; the errors
in its geography and in its dates have been
both seriously and sarcastically reviewed;
and however it is regarded, the fact remains that in the study of saints in Art
St. Ursula cannot be ignored, and in

order to comprehend and enjoy the numerous picturesque representations of this
saint, something must be known of her
legend.

When I began the study of the lives of
the early Christian martyrs, I was under
the impression — and many others have
avowed the same ignorance to me — that
these sufferers were, almost without exception, the poor, to whom the gospel
was preached. But I have learned that
among the comparatively few of whom
we have any knowledge, and among those
who were deemed worthy of canonisation,
a goodly number were of noble, or even
royal, blood.

St. Ursula is still another royal martyr
and saint, daughter of a King of Brittany,
beautiful in person, skilled in accomplish-
ments, and a learned woman withal, charitable, pious, and humble of heart. Her
mother dying while Ursula was still young,

the duties of the first lady of the court fell on her, and her father was quite content when the maiden refused the numerous suitors who desired to marry her.

At length the King of England sent ambassadors to demand the hand of the princess for his son. Ursula saw that her father was much disturbed, as he dared not offend so powerful a sovereign as the ruler of England. Then Ursula proposed that she should answer the ambassadors, which she did by declaring that she would marry Prince Conon on three conditions. First, he should give her as companions ten noble virgins, and to each of these he should give one thousand attendants, and still another thousand to wait on her; second, her marriage should not be consummated until three years had passed, and meantime, with her army of companions, she should visit the shrines sacred to the saints; third, the prince and his court should be baptised into the Christian faith, as Ursula would not wed an unbeliever.

Ursula did not imagine that her conditions would be accepted, but in case they were it would be her blessed lot to save the souls of all these thousands of virgins. To her surprise, the king and his son hastened to fulfil all her conditions, and when the eleven thousand maidens were assembled in Brittany, noblemen from all quarters gathered in great numbers to behold so much youth and beauty dedicated to Christ and a pious pilgrimage.

When all were assembled, Ursula preached to them, and such as had not been baptised now received that rite. Then the princess wrote to Prince Conon, that, having complied with her conditions, he was at liberty to visit her. On his arrival she told him that in a vision she had been bidden to go, with her virgins, to

Rome. At this point the versions of the legend disagree; in some, it is said that Conon remained with her father; others relate that he accompanied the princess and her train on their pilgrimage. All agree that many holy priests, but no sailors, went on the voyage, and the virgins, being taught by heavenly influences, managed the fleet successfully.

They were driven, however, into the harbour of Cologne, where it was miraculously revealed to Ursula that, on their return here, she and all her virgins would suffer martyrdom. This she told to them and they rejoiced, which must have been most disheartening to Prince Conon, if communicated to him.

They at length arrived at Basle and were conducted over the Alps by six angels, finally reaching Rome. The Pope received the virgins with honour, and tents were pitched for them at Tivoli. Here —

however he had come — Conon appeared, and, kneeling with Ursula and being blessed by the Pope, the prince declared that he no longer wished for anything except to share the martyrdom of the princess, and he changed his name to Ethereus, as symbolical of his complete regeneration.

Having visited the shrines of Rome, Ursula prepared to return, and Pope Cyriacus determined to accompany her, in spite of the objections of his clergy, for he had been directed to do so by an angel.

The sight of this great company alarmed the barbarian captains of the troops in Germania, and they feared that the safe return of these virgins to Brittany would lead to the conversion of the whole empire to Christianity. Therefore a command was sent to the King of the Huns, who was then besieging Cologne, and, on the arrival of Ursula and her followers, all except herself were slain. She was led before the prince of the barbarians, who, charmed by her beauty, desired to marry her, and when she indignantly refused he was furious, and shot her with arrows.

In devotional pictures the symbols of St. Ursula are the banner of victory as a Christian; the staff as a pilgrim; the arrow as a martyr; the crown as a princess; and frequently a dove, because it is said that a dove revealed the place of her burial to St. Cunibert.

So numerous are the pictures of St. Ursula, especially those by German painters, that it is difficult to choose those of which to speak. The Venetians represented her as a princess rather than a saint, for while they did not omit her symbols, her dress was so gorgeous that the minor details were scarcely noticeable. Carpaccio painted a grand series of eight

CIMA. — MARY MAGDALENE, ST. LUCIA, AND
ST. CATHERINE.

scenes from her life, which are famous in
the history of Art.   These works, formerly
in the chapel of the Scuola di Sant' Or-
sola, are now in the Academy of Venice.
Certainly the inmates of that school were
to be envied a constant companionship
with these remarkable works.

These pictures were executed between
1490 and 1515; in spite of a certain
crudeness, and some features which are
absolutely grotesque, they are wonderful
works.   Kugler calls them "masterly, rich
in motives and character," and even so
critical a critic as Taine finds much to
praise in Carpaccio.   "We find in him
the chastest of mediæval figures, and that
extreme finish, that perfect truthfulness,
that bloom of the Christian conscience
which the following age, more rude and
sensual, is to trample on in its vehe-
mences."

A great variety of objects are represented in these pictures, and they are interesting as a certain kind of record of the life of Venice at the beginning of the sixteenth century. Later Venetian artists followed the style of Carpaccio, who introduced architecture, grand processions, tapestried halls, gorgeous fabrics, and a thousand brilliant and lustrous objects which could only be associated with the life of St. Ursula by an imaginative Venetian painter, who desired to make all his scenes as luxurious and as nearly a golden confusion as might well be. In all these characteristics Carpaccio was surpassed by later artists, by Giorgione, Titian, and Veronese.

In the chapel of the Hospital of the *Sœurs Noires* at Bruges, there are eight small pictures of scenes from the life of St. Ursula. They were formerly attributed to Hans Memling, but are the work of Dierick Stuerbout. They are executed

with great delicacy, and are most interesting as an example of Teutonic art
in the early part of the fifteenth century.   This artist holds an important
place among the followers of the Van
Eycks; his religious subjects were devoutly treated; his heads are so varied in
character as to give an animation and
individuality to his work; his drawing
is good, and his draperies less angular
than those of Jan van Eyck; his colour,
too, excels that of his contemporaries, and
all these qualities render these pictures of
St. Ursula very attractive.

The famous Reliquary of St. Ursula,
in the Hospital of St. John at Bruges —
said to contain an arm of the saint — was
adorned with miniatures in oil by Memling in 1490.   Six events, from the land-
ing of the saint at Cologne to the time
of her death, are represented.   Of these
Kugler says: " These little pictures are

among the very best productions of the
Flemish school. The drawing in these
small figures is much more beautiful than
in the larger examples by the same master: there is nothing in them meagre,
stiff, or angular; the movements are free;
the execution and tone of colour, with
all its softness, very powerful; the expression in the single heads of great
excellence." It is more than thirty years
since I examined this reliquary, but I
have not forgotten the pleasure it gave
me.

There is a very interesting picture of
St. Ursula in the Bologna Gallery, the
work of St. Catherine of Bologna, called
also Santa Caterina de' Vigri, who was
an abbess of a convent of Poor Clares,
and an artist of repute. Her representation of St. Ursula is one of the many
to which I have referred. The saint is
a stately figure and wears her crown.

With both hands she opens her royal, ermine-trimmed cloak, thus disclosing two groups of kneeling virgins, also with crowns, and hands folded in prayer. This picture is in distemper, on a panel.

The altar-piece by Stephan Lothener, in the Cathedral of Cologne, has on a side panel a picture of St. Ursula, with her escort and her virgins, which is very famous. Albert Dürer wrote in his journal that he paid two silver pennies to have this picture unlocked, that he might see it. Meister Stephan died in 1451, and the excellence of this work makes it probable that it was one of his latest pictures.

In the Dresden Gallery is Hans Burgk-mair's Death of St. Ursula. It is an animated scene, and the contrast between the calm resignation of the Christian maiden and the fierce barbarity of her murderers is excellently rendered. Burgkmair, with all his absolute realism, had a feeling for beauty and dignity, as well as for colour, in which he displayed unusual power and depth.

One would suppose that Prince Conon would frequently appear in pictures of St. Ursula, but, on the contrary, those in which he is seen are remarkable for their rarity. Burgkmair introduced him in a picture now at Augsburg, in which he is enthroned with St. Ursula. In Carpaccio's series he is noticeable but twice: on the occasion of his first meet-ing with the princess, and when they kneel together, before the Pope. In the series by Burgkmair, he is important in the scene at Rome alone.

The Church of St. Ursula at Cologne is decorated with an ancient series of frescoes, illustrating the life of the saint, now much injured by repeated retouch-ing, and in the treasury of the church there is a fine Romanesque reliquary of St. Ursula; but the treasure of this church is the alabaster statue of the saint, lying dead, with a dove at her feet; it is very beautiful. It is the work of Johann Lenz and is dated 1658.

No saint has been more honoured in England than *St. Margaret*, where nearly two hundred and fifty churches are dedicated to her. This is partly due, no doubt, to the fact that a queen of Scotland introduced the name to Great Britain, and was herself canonised.

The St. Margaret represented in art was the daughter of a priest of Antioch, and was reared by a Christian nurse, who converted her. The governor of Antioch, attracted by Margaret's beauty, wished to marry her, but she refused him and declared herself to be a servant of Christ. She was deserted by her father and all her friends, and the enraged governor

subjected her to frightful tortures without obtaining a recantation of her declaration. While she was in prison Satan
appeared in the form of a dragon and
sought to terrify her into submission, but
she held a cross before him and he fled.

Another version relates that the dragon
swallowed her, and then burst, and Margaret emerged unhurt. On account of
this circumstance she is reverenced as the
protector of women in childbirth, for whom
she prayed just before her death, in memory of her escape from the great dragon.

Again and again she was tortured, but
her firmness and piety made so many
converts — five thousand being baptised
in a day — that the governor ordered her
to be beheaded.

Devotional pictures of St. Margaret
show her standing on the dragon, holding
a cross, or, as in the famous work by Raphael, in the Louvre, she holds the mar-

tyr's palm, and stands on a wing of the
dragon, a horrid beast with open mouth.
This picture of the beautiful virgin saint
is said to have been presented by Raphael
to Francis I., whose sister was Margaret
of Navarre. While it certainly merits its
fame, the best judges believe it to have
been largely the work of Giulio Romano;
it has, however, been so many times
cleaned and restored that a correct estimate of it can scarcely be made.

We might look for pearls and daisies
in pictures of this saint, since the word
Margaret signifies a pearl, and a daisy
is also a Marguerite; I know of but one,
however, in which the flower appears, —
in the Academy of Siena, — and although
pearls are rare, I have seen them twined
about the head of St. Margaret.

In the Belvedere, Vienna, is a St. Margaret avowedly by Giulio Romano. It is
quite unlike that in the Louvre. The

face is seen in profile, and a crucifix is in
the hand. The works of Romano are
reminders of Raphael, but have no trace
of the genius of the great master.

A St. Margaret painted by Titian in
1552 is in the Madrid Museum; it was
sent to Philip of Spain. It represents a
fair, beautiful, young maiden, who holds
a cross before a dragon about to emerge
from a cavern.

Niccolo Poussin painted an original
conception of St. Margaret, now in the
Gallery of Turin. The saint kneels on
the dragon while two angels crown her.
The crown distinguishes St. Margaret
from St. Martha, who is represented with
a cross and a dragon.

Besides these celebrated Virgin Patronesses there are the so-called *Great Virgins of the Latin Church*, the difference
between them being that, while the Patronesses are honoured universally, the

veneration of SS. Cecilia, Agnes, Agatha, and Lucia is confined almost entirely to the Western or Latin Church.

The legend of St. Cecilia can, however, be traced back to the third century, the time when she is believed to have lived. It is impossible to separate the actual story of her life from the poetic and marvellous incidents which have been added to it, but it is true, beyond a reasonable doubt, that she lived in Rome, in the time of Alexander Severus, and was reared in the Christian faith from her infancy. She made a vow of celibacy and service to Christ; she excelled in music, wrote hymns, invented the organ, and sang with so heavenly a voice and manner, that it was said that angels were fain to listen to her and to sing with her.

When still very young she was married to Valerian, a young noble of high rank and great wealth.

Cecilia consented to this marriage in obedience to her parents, but beneath her bridal dress she wore a penitential robe, and determined, with God's help, to retain her chastity. She converted Valerian to Christianity, and after his baptism he returned to Cecilia to find an angel with her, who had brought two crowns, made from the roses of Paradise, which he placed on the heads of the young husband and wife. These roses were fresh and fragrant, and invisible to all save the Christian believers.

The "Second Nonnes Tale" of Chaucer gives the legend of St. Cecilia with but little variation from the accepted form.

Valerian prayed to the angel that his brother Tibertius might become a Christian, and this prayer being answered, Cecilia, with the two brothers, went about doing good to the poor, and made many converts. When this was known to the authorities, Valerian and Tibertius were put to death, and Cecilia, after great persecution, died from the effect of wounds and suffering.

At her request her home became a place for Christian worship. A church was built over it, and has been again and again rebuilt, yet it is believed that portions of the original house still exist, and that her bones repose in a silver shrine beneath the altar, near which is the celebrated statue of St. Cecilia lying dead, by Stefano Maderno. This statue was made after the body of the saint was exhumed in 1599, and is intended to represent the appearance and attitude of the remains when her sarcophagus was opened; it is pathetic in its simplicity and repays examination by the visitor to St. Cecilia-in-Trastevere.

In the apse is an ancient mosaic, dating from the early decades of the ninth cen-

tury, which represents SS. Cecilia and
Valerian with a group of other saints,
surrounding the Saviour, who gives them
his benediction.

St. Cecilia was not considered as the
patroness of music *par excellence* until
the fifteenth century, and not until then
were musical instruments seen in all pictures of this saint. She is easily recognised by these, but her other attributes —
roses, an attending angel, and a palm —
belong also to St. Dorothea, which makes
the musical instruments a necessity in
representations of St. Cecilia.

It is not possible to speak of any other
representation of this saint before that by
Raphael in the Bologna Gallery, and of
this picture and its meaning Passavant's
description is most interesting. He
says:

"A sudden inspiration called forth this
picture, and it was in one of his most in-

RAPHAEL. — THE ECSTASY OF ST. CECILIA.

spired moments that the master composed
this exquisite painting. Everything in it
speaks of faith and zeal. All the noble
countenances bear the divine stamp, and
yet, whatever may be the exultation of
their souls, their attitudes are full of the
calmest majesty.

"St. Paul, leaning on a naked sword,
represents knowledge and wisdom, whilst
on the other side St. John shows the full
blessing of divine love. Mary Magdalene,
holding a vase of perfumes, is opposite to
St. Paul, as if to indicate that, if the repentance of the apostle, and his unwearied
activity in the Church, obtained forgiveness for him for his former sins, she also
had been forgiven much because she had
loved much. And as St. Paul, converted
through a vision, is by the side of the
loving St. John, so St. Augustine, also
converted to the faith of Christ, is by the
side of the Magdalene.

" Surrounded by these great and touching figures, St. Cecilia is standing, radiant with ecstasy, listening to the divine harmonies sung by the angels in heaven. The earthly organ falls from her hands, she trembles with holy enthusiasm, and her soul seems longing to fly away to the heavenly country.

" The beauty of the style, and the depth of expression are not the only things that render this a masterpiece; but the combination of these with harmony, richness, and powerful colouring. The colouring responds to the poetry of the subject; it carries us into an ethereal and mysterious atmosphere. No colourist has ever equalled this splendour, which we may call almost divine. Titian's Assumption excites feelings of joyfulness, Correggio's St. Jerome a gentle emotion, but Raphael's St. Cecilia brings us nearer to heaven."

A goodly number of both Italian and German masters have put their ideal of St. Cecilia on canvas; Domenichino painted six single figures of her as a patron saint; Moretto, two, while Garofalo, Giulio Campi, and others represented her according to their conceptions.

The angel crowning Cecilia and Valerian and the death of Cecilia are the historical scenes most frequently represented singly, but several series illustrative of her life have been painted. Two scenes from such a series, believed to be the work of Byzantine masters in the ninth century, are in the church in Rome, above mentioned. They are at the right of the high altar, and are most interesting examples of their school and era.

A very early series, by Cimabue, is in the Academy of Florence. The picture of the saint enthroned was originally an altar-piece, and is surrounded by eight small pictures of scenes in her life. A series by Francia and Lorenzo Costa, in Bologna, is very much injured. They were originally in a chapel, but through a succession of changes they are now in a passage between two streets. The little that remains of them is most interesting and proves them to have been very beautiful. Five scenes from a series by Pinturicchio are in the Berlin Gallery.

Domenichino, in addition to the single figures already mentioned, executed four historical scenes in a chapel of St. Cecilia, in the Church of San Luigi de' Francesi, in Rome. The subjects here are the Angel offering the Crowns, Cecilia's contempt for Idols, her Distribution of her clothes among the poor, her Death and Apotheosis, which last is on the ceiling. There is much to admire in these works, and, alas! much that is incongruous with the subjects and the place for which they were painted. They are, however, good examples of the work of Domenichino, whose treatment was frequently theatrical. He often allowed the details to detract from the principal motive of his picture ; for example, in the scene in which the saint distributes her goods to the poor, it is not Cecilia who holds the attention, but the group of poor people below who struggle for the gifts thrown from the balcony above, and who are most powerfully represented. In the scene of the death, where the wounded saint is most attractive and pathetic, two women wiping up her blood are exasperating in their distraction of one's thoughts and in the repulsiveness of their occupation. Such details are better omitted, but Domenichino was not sensitive himself, nor did he consider this quality in others, but he was the best artist of the Caracci school and admirable in his expression and colour. The Apotheosis of St. Cecilia is lovely in design; the saint is borne to heaven by angels who also carry her organ, palm, sword, and crown.

We have more historical authority for the story of *St. Agnes* than exists in many cases. St. Jerome wrote of her as being greatly venerated in his day, and her legend is one of the oldest saintly narratives. The principal facts are that St. Agnes lived in Rome and was a most beautiful Christian maiden; when still very young she vowed never to marry. A young nobleman, who sought her hand, when rejected became ill unto death, so great was his disappointment. When his father, the Prefect Sempronius, learned the truth, he used every possible effort to persuade Agnes to reconsider her refusal, and when she would not, the prefect became angry and commanded Agnes to be stripped of her clothing and exposed to all possible disgrace. When this was done, her already abundant hair so increased as to perfectly veil her person. Her persecutors were so confounded by this miracle that they locked her in a room alone, and when she prayed she beheld a shining garment before her, in which she clothed herself.

Then her lover, hoping that she would now listen to his pleading, came into the chamber, which was illumined with heavenly light, and so soon as he entered he was struck with blindness and fell down in convulsions, and Agnes, being filled with compassion, prayed for his restoration, which prayer was speedily answered.

Sempronius, on beholding this, would have saved the maiden from further sorrow, but the people declared that she was a sorceress, and when she protested that she was simply a Christian maiden, they piled fagots around her, and set them on fire. But the flames did her no harm, while some of her tormentors were slain by them. She at length met her death by the sword, and her remains were entombed in a cemetery, to which the Christians constantly went to pray at her grave.

At length, as her parents and friends were paying their devotions at her tomb, she appeared to them in a glorified form, and beside her was a lamb of a whiteness purer than snow. Agnes assured her friends of her perfect happiness, and again vanished, and from this time they no more mourned her death, but rejoiced at her safety.

In the most ancient representations of St. Agnes the lamb is not present, but I know of no picture of importance from which it is absent. Titian's picture, in the Louvre, shows the saint in the act of presenting her martyr's palm to Christ.

ALONZO CANO. — ST. AGNES.

In the Academy of Venice a picture by Veronese represents the saint, as the patroness of celibacy, in the act of presenting a young nun to the Madonna, and as the patron of maidens St. Agnes is especially lovely; these works are rich in the glorious Venetian colouring.

When we consider the story of St. Agnes it seems like madness in Andrea del Sarto to have painted a portrait of his wife, who was the opposite of Agnes in character, as the lovely maiden saint; the picture in the Cathedral of Pisa is, however, an exquisite work. The saint is seated and embraces the lamb with her left hand, while she raises the martyr's palm with the right, and gazes upward with an expression of peaceful trust. The veil encircles the head within the aureole; the violet and amber of the drapery are charming, and the whole picture is admirable.

The Martyrdom of St. Agnes, by Domenichino, now in the Bologna Gallery, is
a distressing picture, the moment represented being that in which a brutal executioner seizes her hair, and with it draws
her head back, and plunges a sword into
her bosom; when observing it one is in-
dignant that the spectators do not fly
from such a scene, and that the angels
above do not throw down their musical
instruments and weep, rather than utter
sweet sounds so calmly as they seem to
be doing.

In delightful contrast is Tintoretto's
picture of the same subject in the Church
of Santa Maria dell' Orto, Venice.   Here
the sweet girl saint, in pure white drapery,
kneels at the summit of a flight of steps,
awaiting the stroke of the executioner.
It is most dramatic in design and effect,
and as attractive as a picture of this
especial moment could be made.

The story of *St. Agatha* is so painful, and her martyrdom included such horrors, that it is not necessary to recount them. The picture by Sebastian del Piombo, in the Pitti, and others which represent the tearing of the breasts, are too revolting for description; in truth, I could never so study them as to be able to write of them. In a few cases the saint is seen bound to a cross or column, nude to the waist, and the executioners with their pincers standing by.

The symbols of St. Agatha are the palm, cross, and shears; she is sometimes holding a salver on which is a female breast; she wears a long veil and is of dignified and even majestic bearing. She is a protector against fire and all diseases of the breast, and patroness of Malta and Catania.

St. Lucia is patroness of Syracuse, Sicily, and of the labouring poor, and a protector against diseases of the eye.

One legend of her life and death makes no mention of her eyes, but another, which has been followed by artists, relates that, as a young man whose love she had rejected declared that he was bewitched by her eyes, she took them out and sent them to her lover, begging that, as he now had what he had so much desired, he would henceforth leave her in peace. But God did not permit Lucia to remain sightless, and so restored her eyes that they were more beautiful than before.

In devotional pictures, St. Lucia is frequently seen carrying her eyes on a salver, but far more beautiful is the picture of this saint richly dressed, and bearing a lamp in one hand — the symbol of celestial light and wisdom — and the palm in the other; by this symbol the meaning of her name, light, is far more artistically indicated. After her persecutions, Lucia died from a wound in her throat from a poniard

CARLO DOLCI - ST. LUCIA.

or sword, as appears in a picture in the Uffizi, by Carlo Dolci.

A St. Lucia by Baroccio is in the Louvre, in which the saint presents her palm to the Madonna, while an attendant angel bears her eyes. Palma painted the apotheosis of St. Lucia, in the church in Venice which is dedicated to her. It represents the saint as borne to heaven in a glory of angels, one of them carrying her eyes.

This saint should be represented as illuminated with heavenly light, — with wisdom and sweetness, as Dante speaks of her, " Lucia, of all cruelty the foe."

St. Lucia is dear to the people of Sicily, and to Naples especially, and one cannot be long in Southern Italy without becoming familiar with her; she is loved for her purity and gentleness, such as Fra Angelico painted in his picture now in the Academy of Siena.

CHAPTER VII.

OTHER SAINTS IMPORTANT IN ART.

AS the first Christian martyr, *St. Stephen* commands especial reverence. In the sixth chapter of the Acts of the Apostles we read that he was "full of faith and of the Holy Ghost;" that he "did great wonders and miracles among the people;" that when "certain of the synagogue" could not resist his wisdom and spirit, false witnesses were suborned to accuse him of blasphemy, and he was stoned to death, even while praying for his murderers, "Lord, lay not this sin to their charge."

The legend of St. Stephen relates the discovery of his remains alone, and says

that four hundred years after his death,
by means of a miraculous dream, his relics
were found in the tomb of Gamaliel, and
were deposited in the Church of Sion, at
Jerusalem. Later they were carried to
Constantinople, and then to Rome, where
they were placed beside those of St. Lawrence. It is related that when the remains of St. Stephen were placed in the
sarcophagus, St. Lawrence moved to the
left, leaving the right to St. Stephen, for
which deferential act St. Lawrence is frequently called " the courteous Spaniard."

On account of this legend SS. Stephen
and Lawrence are often seen in the
same pictures, in which St. Stephen is
distinguished from St. Lawrence, or from
other saints habited as deacons, by stones,
or by wounds on his head. Devotional
pictures almost invariably present St.
Stephen in the dress of a deacon, rich
with sumptuous embroidery and heavy

gold tassels. His symbols are the palm and the Gospel, and stones are at his feet or on his head and shoulders, as in a picture in the Brera, Milan, by Carpaccio.

The text, " They saw his face as it had been the face of an angel," is the warrant for picturing St. Stephen as young; and the gentle, calm expression usually given to representations of him is in accord with his forgiveness of his persecutors. In Spanish pictures he is sometimes an older man. In the Berlin Museum, a picture of SS. Stephen and John the Baptist, by Francesco Francia, is interesting and is an example of the best manner of this excellent imitator of Perugino and Raphael.

The Martyrdom of St. Stephen has been many times represented, and is a subject that can scarcely be mistaken. The picture by Tintoretto, in the Church

of San Giorgio Maggiore, Venice, presents
the saint kneeling in the foreground; the
air is full of flying stones, and the ground
covered with those that have fallen; he
wears the rich dress of a prelate, and his
countenance is perfectly serene; beside
him is a book, the law of Moses, which
Stephen had expounded, and which the
Jews violated in thus stoning Stephen.
In the upper part of the picture, the
Almighty, Christ, and St. Michael appear.
In the middle distance is a motley crowd,
three or four men furiously throwing
stones.

Almost exactly in the centre of the
picture St. Paul is seated on the ground,
with loose garments thrown across his
knees; he is a noble, calm figure, his
dress being red and black, as is the
drapery of the Almighty, which renders
these two figures the colour centres of
the scene. Of this picture Ruskin says:

" It is almost impossible to praise too highly the refinement of conception which withdrew the unconverted St. Paul into the distance, so as entirely to separate him from the immediate interest of the scene, and yet marked the dignity to which he was afterward to be raised, by investing him with the colours which occurred nowhere else in the picture except in the dress which veils the form of the Godhead. . . . It is also worth observing how boldly imaginative is the treatment which covers the ground with piles of stones, and yet leaves the martyr apparently untouched. Another painter would have covered him with blood, and elaborated the expression of pain upon his countenance. Tintoretto leaves us under no doubt as to what manner of death he is dying; he makes the air hurtle with the stones, but he does not choose to make his picture disgusting,

or even painful. The face of the martyr
is serene and exulting, and we leave the
picture remembering only how 'he fell
asleep.'"

In the Royal Gallery at Nuremburg
are pictures of the Martyrdom and of
the scene when St. Stephen was before
the High Priest. They are by Albrecht
Altdorfer, a pupil and imitator of Albert
Dürer, and are good and interesting examples of the German school of the
sixteenth century.

Cigoli's Martyrdom of St. Stephen is in
the Uffizi; it is spirited and most
pathetic, but the unnecessary ferocity
of the stone throwers is extremely painful. Le Brun's picture of the same scene,
in the Louvre, is doubtless his masterpiece. It is as quiet in effect as is possible to such a subject. The moment
represented is that when St. Stephen is
dying; the executioners are watching his

face, which is turned toward heaven with
an expression of trustful submission.

In the Hermitage, St. Petersburg, is
Pietro da Cortona's picture of this martyrdom. The works of this master are
startling in colour and dazzling in the
management of lights, which qualities are
not well suited to pathetic and religious
subjects; however, his originality in the
conception of his pictures makes them
very interesting.

The scenes in the life of the protomar-
tyr, together with those in the life of St.
Lawrence, were painted by Fra Angelico,
on the walls of the chapel of Nicolas V.,
in the Vatican. A series by Carpaccio
is scattered, the Consecration as Deacon
being in the Berlin Gallery, the Preaching
of St. Stephen in the Louvre, and the
Dispute with the Doctors in the Brera.

In the Madrid Museum there are six
scenes of similar subjects by Juan Juanes,

which are admirable examples of the work
of this imitator of Raphael, who still retained the peculiar characteristics of the
Spanish school. He painted religious subjects only, and, like Angelico, began them
with prayer and fasting. The colour in
the pictures of Juanes is most satisfactory,
and he was original in the composition of
his works, but there is a severity in all
he did which corresponds to his personal
character.

St. Lawrence and St. Stephen have been
so intimately associated in Art and in legend that one is prone to associate them
in thought, yet St. Lawrence lived more
than two centuries later than St. Stephen,
and the circumstances in the lives of these
young deacons were totally different. St.
Lawrence was a Spaniard who went to
Rome and was chosen as his deacon by
Sixtus II. After the martyrdom of the
Pope, Lawrence, to whom the treasures

of the Church had been confided, went through the city, distributing them to the poor and suffering. When this was known to the prefect, he could not by any means persuade the young deacon to tell him where the treasures of the Church were hidden. When thus questioned, Lawrence simply pointed to the sick and poor, and declared them to be the treasures of Christ's Church. At length the prefect gave him over to the executioners, and sentenced him to be roasted alive on a bed made of iron bars, like a gridiron.

St. Lawrence is a most important saint. In Spain the Escurial is dedicated to him; in Rome six churches are known by his name; the Cathedral of Genoa is sacred to him, and, in short, there is rarely a city or town in Christendom which has not consecrated a monument to him, England having about two hundred and fifty churches called by his name.

Devotional pictures of St. Lawrence are almost numberless, and when the gridiron is present as his symbol, they cannot be mistaken. He wears the dress of a deacon, and his other emblems are the cross, the palm, a book, a censer, or a dish full of coins. The gridiron is rarely absent, and when not large and absolutely prominent, a miniature one is frequently suspended by a chain around his neck, or embroidered on his robe.

Titian's picture of the Martyrdom of St. Lawrence, painted for Philip II., to be placed in the Escurial, is famous, as well as a second of the same subject now in the Gesuiti, Venice. Such night scenes require a good light, which, unfortunately, these have not, and both are blackened by age and smoke. They are wonderfully dramatic, and are remarkable for the grandeur of their composition, as well as for the exactness of the anatomical drawing, and seem to unite the pictorial talent of the great Venetian with the sculptural genius of Michael Angelo.

The picture of the Charity of St. Lawrence by Fra Angelico, in the series mentioned above, is very attractive. The saint is in a rich dress, and has a large aureole about his head; his eyes are cast down as if carefully choosing his path, and in one hand he holds a money bag.

St. Hippolytus, who is frequently introduced in pictures of St. Lawrence, was a soldier whose duty it was to guard the saint at the time of his terrible death. The wonderful faith and constancy of St. Lawrence converted Hippolytus to Christianity, and he in turn suffered a frightful death, being tied to the tails of wild horses. These saints are naturally companions in works of art. A picture of the martyrdom of St. Hippolytus, by Subleyras, now in the Louvre, is very effective. The saint is on the ground, tied to two horses, which are held with difficulty by a group of soldiers. The head of the saint and the expression of his face as he gazes heavenward are very fine.

The Bible story of *St. Mary Magdalene* is too well known to require repetition here, but there are many curious legends connected with her. That which relates that after the Ascension of Christ she came to France, and after preaching to the people, making many converts, and seeing her brother Lazarus established as Bishop of Marseilles, she retired to a desert and devoted thirty years to severe penance for her past sins, is the foundation of the well-known and numerous pictures of the Penitent Magdalene. She is frequently represented as a patron saint, is many times introduced as a worshipper

of the Infant Jesus in Madonna pictures;
she is present in the scenes connected
with the life and death of Our Lord, as
related in the New Testament, as well as
in some legendary subjects. The Magdalene is the patroness of Provence, and also
of sinning and repentant women.

Her special symbol is the box of ointment, and she is rarely represented without
it; this is much varied in size and shape,
is sometimes in her hand, and again is
placed near her, and in some cases is
carried by an attendant angel. When
pictured as a penitent, the cross, skull,
and scourge are introduced, as well as a
crown of thorns, the latter being sometimes presented to the saint by an angel.

The Magdalenes of Spanish pictures are
frequently dark haired, but the abundant
blonde or golden-tinted hair is that which
is customarily seen. Her draperies are
red when her passionate love is expressed,

and blue or violet when penitence or mourning are indicated; when red and violet are present, both love and sorrow are symbolised.

In the early pictures of the Magdalene as the patroness of erring women, she is emaciated, and most unattractive, being frequently nude except that her hair is like a cloak about her. A very ancient picture of this type is in the Academy of Florence, and above the altar dedicated to her, in the Baptistery of the same city, is the famous statue carved in wood by Donatello. It is painful, and almost repulsive in its realism, and intensely expressive of grief and severe penance.

As time passed, this representation was abandoned, and gradually the Magdalene became a beautiful woman, magnificently attired, with no traces of suffering, dignified and gracious, with the precious ointment ever in her hand, or very near her.

It has been more than once suggested that many pictures of the Magdalene and her alabaster box would as well represent Pandora, except for the aureole which is always given to the saint. Several Magdalenes of this character, by Guido Reni and other painters of the Caracci school, are seen in European collections.

The Magdalene of Raphael, in the famous picture of St. Cecilia in Bologna, is a graceful figure, and her face is sweet and gentle in expression. In this work she is opposite St. Paul; she has been represented with SS. Peter and Jerome, and even with the Prophet Isaiah; in such pictures the Magdalene may be considered as suggestive of love as these others are of the power of the spirit.

In Correggio's celebrated Madonna in the Gallery of Parma, called The Day, — because of the diffusion of the pure, radiant daylight, in contrast with the

artificial lights in The Night, at Dresden,
— the Magdalene kisses the foot of the
child, and an angel near her bears the box
of ointment. This picture is also known
as the Madonna of St. Jerome, as that
saint is standing near the Virgin.

Pictures of the repentant Magdalene
vary greatly in expression, and Mrs.
Jameson well says : " We have Magdalenes who look as if they never could
have sinned, and others who look as if
they never could have repented; we have
Venetian Magdalenes with the air of cour-
tesans, and Florentine Magdalenes with
the air of Ariadnes; and Bolognese Magdalenes like sentimental Niobes; and
French Magdalenes, *moitié galantes, moitié
devotes ;* and Dutch Magdalenes who wring
their hands like repentant washerwomen.
The Magdalenes of Rubens remind us of
nothing so much as of the 'unfortunate
Miss Bailey;' and the Magdalenes of Van-

dyck are fine ladies who have turned
Methodists. But Mary Magdalene, such
as we have conceived her, mournful, yet
hopeful, tender, yet dignified, worn with
grief and fasting, yet radiant with the
glow of love and faith, and clothed with
the beauty of holiness, is an ideal which
painting has not yet realised. Is it beyond the reach of Art?"

Oëlenschläger called the Reading Penitent Magdalene, by Correggio, in the
Dresden Gallery, "The Goddess of the
Religious Solitude," and by all who have
seen the picture itself, or are familiar
with it by means of good reproductions,
I fancy it is more frequently recalled than
any other of the numerous pictures of
this subject, and to many it is the only
one worthy of remembrance.

The Magdalene which Titian painted
for Charles V. is a most dramatic work.
The penitent has one hand on her breast

and the other resting on a skull; her
golden hair floats all about her shoulders;
her tearful eyes are raised to heaven; a
book and the box of ointment are near
her on a rock, and the whole composition
is thrown into full relief by a desolate
background and jagged rocks. This was
so much admired that the master and his
pupils repeated it, and Titian boasted of
the money he had made from this subject.
One of these replicas is in the Pitti, one
in the Doria Gallery, Rome, one in the
Museum of Naples, and still another in
the Hermitage, St. Petersburg.

The Magdalenes of Guido Reni are
lovely pictures of a beautiful woman in
low spirits, but are quite innocent of any
religious or spiritual elements or expression. Two Magdalenes by Guido are in
the Louvre, where is Murillo's Magdalene
also. By the latter she is represented
kneeling in prayer, with the hands crossed

on the breast; the crucifix, skull, book, and alabaster box are all near her. It is a far more satisfactory portrayal of devout repentance and perfect trust than is often expressed in Art. The whole work is sincere and simple in the extreme.

The Magdalenes by Rubens and Vandyck are too numerous to be catalogued here, since the subject of these pictures is easily recognised. In Rubens' so-called Four Penitents, in the Munich Gallery, we see a Magdalene of profound humility, pure pathos, and tender love, wonderfully painted. The other penitents are David, Peter, and the Penitent Thief. Vandyck's picture of the same subject is in the gallery at Augsburg.

The personal characteristics and the symbols of the Magdalene are so pronounced that she can scarcely fail to be recognised, even in illustrations of Scriptural subjects in which she is one of a group; for example, the Supper at the House of Simon; Christ at the Home of Martha and Mary; the Raising of Lazarus; the Crucifixion, and the Descent from the Cross; the Marys at the Sepulchre; and the picture known as the *Noli me tangere*, — touch me not, — which shows the Saviour with Mary Magdalene after his resurrection.

The Supper at the House of Simon has been represented in every possible manner, from the most simple composition by Taddeo Gaddi in the Rinuccini Chapel, Florence, to the magnificent banqueting scene by Veronese, in the Turin Gallery, which is a splendid example of the gorgeous pictures which this master loved to paint.

In quite another manner Mabuse represented this Supper, and made it as elaborate as any Venetian could desire, and yet its effect is a striking example of the

difference between the style of the Flemish and Venetian schools. This work is
now in the Brussels Museum. The architecture of the picture is elaborately ornate ;
every bit of space is covered with ornament of some kind, while the arrangement
of double staircases and openings into
several apartments gives the house of
Simon the appearance of spaciousness.
In the banqueting-hall are two tables,
sitting at one of which are Jesus, Simon,
and another, probably "the disciple whom
Jesus loved." The Magdalene is about to
kiss the foot of our Lord ; her jar of ointment is beside her; her posture is that of
great humility, and she is largely concealed by the table beneath which she
crouches. Jesus has his hand raised, and
is answering Judas, who objects to the
waste of the ointment: "Let her alone:
against the day of my burying hath she
kept this. For the poor always ye have

ROSSETTI. — MARY MAGDALENE AT THE HOUSE
OF SIMON.

with you; but me ye have not always."
Simon is a dignified man, richly dressed.
At a second table a number of guests are
seated, and glimpses into other rooms
show servants moving about. This picture bears out the words of Kugler, who
says that Mabuse, before going to Italy,
was one of the first artists of the Van
Eyck school, "displaying great knowledge
of composition, able drawing, warm colouring, an unusual mastery in the management of the brush, and a solidity in the
carrying out of every portion such as few
of his contemporaries attained. His only
deficiency consists sometimes in a certain
coldness of religious feeling."

The picture of the Magdalene at the
House of Simon, by Dante Gabriel Rossetti, is an especially interesting work.
Here it is the outside of the house that
is seen, and the Magdalene is making her
way up the steps to the entrance, through

a crowd of people, all of whom are intently
watching her, and of whom she seems
unconscious, her whole attention being
fixed on what she can see through the
open door of the supper-room.

The manner of the people in this crowd
plainly shows that they consider the Magdalene one to be stared and even leered at
in the most insolent manner; but all this
now means nothing to her. She knows
that Jesus is within the house she is about
to enter, and it is of him alone that she
thinks; she has left her past behind her
and is pressing forward in the new path
which Jesus has opened to her.

We can see in the picture what she
cannot, since Jesus at a window is visible
to us, and she can only see those who sat
at meat with him. One of these, a gross
looking man, near the door, regards her
scornfully, while an attendant behind him
views her approach with curiosity.

The face of the Magdalene is beautiful, and full of a fixed purpose. She tears the flowers from her hair, which is streaming about her shoulders; the box of ointment hangs from her girdle.

The details of the picture are numerous. In the lower corner of the work, beneath the window where Jesus is seen, a lamb — emblem of innocence and of sacrifice — is eating of the flowers which grow abundantly.

The draperies on the two prominent figures at the side of the steps, in the foreground, have a tapestry effect, and are very rich; this pair seem like a gay youth and his mistress — suggested by the familiar and disrespectful manner in which he places his hands on her foot and knee — who have known the Magdalene in another phase of her life, and regard her with scornful surprise in this, her new character.

The beggar girl sitting on the lower step is a beautiful and effective figure. She turns from her bowl of food, holding her spoon in one hand, and lifts her face above her shoulder, looking up at the Magdalene; thus she reveals her own attractive features and her luxuriant hair, and makes one tremble for her future when her surroundings are considered, for the men and women in the street below and beyond the Magdalene are not such as this child should be exposed to. Quite in the background musicians are playing, and through an opening figures are seen, gradually growing indistinct in the distance.

Christ at the house of Martha and Mary has also been variously represented by painters of religious subjects. In some pictures the house, the sisters, and Lazarus are very commonplace in appearance, and suggest an ordinary labouring family in their home; again the brother and sisters are seen in a luxurious dwelling, with all the accessories of wealth surrounding them.

The legend relates that Martha, who was a Christian, and sadly mourned the life led by her sister, presented the erring Mary to Jesus. An engraving by Marc Antonio Raimondi, after Raphael, — no picture being known to exist of this scene, — represents this presentation, though not in the home of the sisters. Jesus is seated in the pillared entrance to the temple, to which a flight of steps ascends, on which are the sisters, Martha leading Mary and being a little in advance. Martha is looking in her sister's face, and pointing toward Jesus as if to assure her that with him she would find forgiveness and peace. Mary's eyes are cast down while Jesus holds out his hand as if in encouragement and benediction. Near Our Lord is

a group of three men, probably his disciples, and just behind him another, who is
thought by some critics to represent Lazarus, as his regard is fixed on the sisters
intently. In the street below a crowd of
people watch the ascent of Martha and
Mary with great interest. This engraving is in the Louvre, and is not uncom-
mon in other public collections.

Jouvenet's picture of the same subject
is also in the Louvre. Here Mary kneels
before Jesus, who is seated, while Martha,
standing near by, is evidently talking, and
gesticulates with vehemence.

In pictures of the Raising of Lazarus
the two sisters are present and are easily
distinguished. This subject was frequently
represented in the early centuries of Christianity, and was thought a fitting emblem
of the resurrection of the dead as taught
in the Apostles' Creed. It is seen on the
ancient sarcophagi, is one of the series of

RUBENS. — THE RAISING OF LAZARUS.

the miracles of Christ, and is never omitted in scenes from the life of Mary Magdalene.

In the Berlin Museum is the picture of this miracle by Rubens. Lazarus, who emerges from the tomb on one side, is already partly freed from his cerements and has his eyes fixed on the face of Our Lord, who, standing on the opposite side of the picture, raises his hands in benediction. Lazarus is apparently unconscious of the presence of his sisters, who kneel between him and Jesus.

Mary regards her brother earnestly and is busy unwinding still more of the grave-clothes, while Martha, looking up to Jesus, raises her hands in awe and amazement. Two men are behind this group, one of them looking at Lazarus attentively, while the other assists in removing the winding-sheet.

A criticism has been made of this picture because Mary is evidently thinking only of her brother, for the moment forgetful of Jesus, as if more vitally interested in the restoration of Lazarus than in the power which had effected it. This is very human, as Rubens was accustomed to be, but this scene is not usually so represented.

The picture by Fra Angelico, in the Academy of Florence, is remarkable for its directness and simplicity. At the command of Christ, Lazarus, wrapped in grave-clothes, comes forth from his tomb; his hands are clasped as he looks at Jesus, before whom his sisters are kneeling; behind Christ is a group of four figures, and near Lazarus are two others, one of whom covers his nose with his hands. Giotto, in his picture in the Arena Chapel, Padua, makes this reference to the truth that Lazarus had been actually dead less disagreeably suggestive, by representing those nearest the risen man with their robes wrapped over their faces below the eyes.

Tintoretto's picture in the Scuola di San Rocco, Venice, is not so fine a work as one would expect to see from the hand of this master. In the lower portion Christ is in a half-reclining position; in the upper part the grave-clothes are being taken off Lazarus; a group of spectators exhibit neither awe nor surprise; they are apparently as calm as if the dead were raised in their sight daily.

Naturally, the most interesting picture of this subject is that by Sebastian del Piombo, in the National Gallery. The accepted story of this work is that, when Cardinal Giulio dei Medici commissioned Raphael to paint the Transfiguration, he also gave an order to Sebastian to paint a companion in size, representing the Raising of Lazarus. Michael Angelo being in Rome, and, as it is said, sympathising

with Sebastian in his dislike of Raphael
and jealousy of his fame, determined to
aid Sebastian, and made a design for the
picture which Del Piombo coloured. The
Lazarus is believed to have been thus produced. It is one of the most important
and interesting pictures of the sixteenth
century.

The moment chosen is after Lazarus
has left the tomb; he is seated on a sarcophagus in the right centre of the picture,
while his grave-clothes are being removed
by others. Christ stands in the centre,
and, with one hand raised, he points
toward Lazarus with the other; he is
evidently speaking, and various words
have been attributed to this moment by
different critics; to me it seems that he
is uttering the command, "Loose him,
and let him go." The figure of Christ
is artistically inferior to the rest of the
work. At his feet Mary Magdalene is

kneeling, and gazes in the face of the Master with faith and gratitude, while Martha stands on one side, turning her face away, as if afraid to look at the risen Lazarus.

Many figures surround the principal personages in the scene, all expressing astonishment and curiosity. The background represents Jerusalem, and a bridge above a river, in which a group of women are washing linen; in the middle ground is a huge tree, the top of which is cut off by the size of the canvas. One may well study the draperies and all the different details of the figures, which are wonderfully modelled. The light and shade, too, are fine, parts of the picture being in shadow, while other portions are brilliant with sunshine.

We are so accustomed to see the Magdalene at the foot of the cross in pictures of the Crucifixion — a representation said

to have originated with Giotto — that it
is scarcely needful to speak of it; in some
cases she embraces the cross; the box of
ointment is frequently near her, in order
that she may be distinguished from the
Virgin and the third Mary.

I have studied the Crucifixion by Rubens, in the Antwerp Cathedral, many
times, and admire it beyond all other
representations of this subject, but have
always regretted that the Magdalene, with
her arms around the cross, does not look
at Jesus rather than at the executioner.
By this regard of the saint Rubens gave
himself an opportunity for a remarkable
expression of detestation and horror on
her face, but the more one studies the
picture and realises the full meaning of
the scene, the greater is the surprise that
in this supreme moment the Magdalene
could have realised the presence of any
other than Our Lord.

Vandyck painted several Crucifixions; one is in the Cathedral of Mechlin; one in Vienna, in the Belvedere; and a third in the Museum of Antwerp. Vandyck's pictures of this and kindred subjects are full of profound emotion, and of an intense and elevated expression of religious faith and love. In the Crucifixion, the passionate feeling which he depicts in the face, figure, and action of the Magdalene is in striking contrast to the profound and patient pathos which he imparts to the Virgin.

In some pictures of the Crucifixion, the Descent from the Cross, and the Entombment, the Virgin faints in the arms of the Magdalene. At other times this saint is weeping, or embracing the feet she once anointed, as is the case in a design for a window made by the late Sir Edward Burne-Jones, in which Jesus is seated above the Magdalene, and she, with great humility, embraces his feet.

In the Pietà the Magdalene is often a conspicuous figure, as in pictures of this subject by Fra Bartolommeo and Andrea del Sarto, both in the Pitti; in the first she passionately presses the feet of the dead Christ to her bosom while her whole figure speaks the very abandonment of hopeless grief; in the second, she is kneeling and wringing her hands.

The pictures of Mary Magdalene at the Sepulchre, when she is alone, are founded on the account of St. John the Evangelist. In the other Gospels, both two and three women are mentioned, and they frequently appear like representations of the myrrh-bearers of the Greeks, who carried spices and perfumes to the tombs of the dead. This picture is very easily recognised, and I shall speak of but two, one very modern, by Sir Edward Burne-Jones, and a second, by Mantegna, almost four centuries old.

FRA ANGELICO.—JESUS APPEARS TO MARY MAGDALENE.

In the first, two shining angels sit on the empty sarcophagus; between them Mary stands, looking back over her shoulder and lifting her hand in her surprise,—wonderfully expressed both in her face and figure,—at seeing Jesus, although St. John tells us that in this moment she "knew not that it was Jesus." The angels, too, seem greatly moved by his appearance; one, whom Mary has been facing, points to Jesus, and turns his eyes toward him without turning the head; it is apparently the gesture of this angel which has caused Mary to look over her shoulder. John's account does not represent her as entering the sepulchre, only as looking in, and when she turned herself back she saw Jesus. The second angel, nearest to the Lord, looks directly at him, with surprised face, and rests one hand on the sarcophagus and bends slightly, as though drawing away from the risen Christ. Both the angels hold their robes over their mouths with one hand, in a manner which recalls the expression, " the silence of the tomb," and also symbolises a reverence that forbids speech ; each has a flame above the brow, and their wings are folded behind their heads.

Mantegna's picture is in the National Gallery, London. It represents the sarcophagus from which Jesus has risen, on a platform in the midst of rocks which tower behind it. Below this platform there are rude steps cut in the rock itself. One exquisite angel, with wonderful wings, sits on the empty tomb and lifts the grave-clothes from it, as if to show the Magdalene, who stands near by, that there is no body here. She, holding her jar of spices, makes a gesture of surprise. She is a most graceful figure. Meantime the Virgin Mary, and the other Mary, who have been at the foot of the rock, begin

MANTEGNA. — MARY MAGDALENE AT THE
SEPULCHRE.

to ascend, as if to assure themselves of the miracle which has been wrought.

The details of this picture are curious. In the foreground is a bit of water, on which are ducks; a turtle is lying on a small rock, and various small bunches of homely herbage are springing up. It is altogether a quaint and acceptable picture.

There are series of pictures of the life of the Magdalene, founded on extraordinarily wild legends, of which I shall not speak. The colouring, the abundant hair, and the general character of the representations of this saint are such as make her easily recognised. Several such series, like that by Giotto, in the Bargello, Florence, are so much injured as to be ineffective; another series is in the Chapel of the Magdalene at Assisi; and separate scenes occur in the windows of some French cathedrals, as at Bourges and Chartres, while around the porch of the

Certosa, at Pavia, a series of bas-reliefs tells the same story.

The appearance of Jesus to Mary Magdalene in the Garden — known as the *Noli me tangere* — has been many times represented, and is less subject to variation than are many other pictures in the lives of saints. The Scriptural account of this event fixes the scene and the number of persons present, leaving to the artist the choice of their positions and the expression to be given the faces and figures.

This subject did not appeal to the earliest painters, but from the fourteenth century, both in Italy and Germany, its artistic importance was recognised. Much might be said of the manner in which the Christ has been pictured in this scene, many painters making the fatal error of extreme realism and putting a spade in the hand or on the shoulder of Jesus, — a most unhappy allusion to the declaration of St. John that when the Magdalene first beheld the risen Lord she supposed him to be a gardener, — even the spiritual Fra Angelico permitting himself to commit such an error; and when — as in a design which I believe to be wrongly ascribed to Raphael — the figure of Jesus is that of an old labourer, with a large pickaxe on his shoulder, wearing a broad shade hat, beyond which a generous and brilliant aureole appears, one cannot pardon this absurdity, nor even smile at it when connected with so sacred a motive. But these considerations are more suitable to a life of Christ than to one of the Magdalene, who, in these works, with few exceptions, is properly represented. She is adoring and humble, and as one looks at a fitting picture of the scene he wonders why Jesus should have denied the saint that touch which would have assured her of his identity as it later removed the doubts of Thomas. Was it not a recognition of her greater faith? and was she not thus included among those of whom he spake when he said: "Thomas, because thou hast seen me, thou hast believed: blessed are they that have not seen, and yet have believed?"

Lorenzo di Credi, in his picture in the Uffizi, painted a sweet and loving Magdalene, but one who scarcely represents a woman who has sinned and repented, and shown such force of character as had Mary Magdalene. Titian, in his picture in the National Gallery, has depicted a most beautiful woman, with more of the earnestness and energy which belong to this saint.

Baroccio, in his picture in the Uffizi, has represented the moment of the recognition of Jesus by Mary; she has knelt in order to look into the sepulchre, and, hearing the one word, "Mary," she has turned to exclaim, "Rabboni."

The picture by Angelico, in the Museum of San Marco, Florence, represents a later moment. The scene is a garden; on one side is the opening of the tomb, from which, not finding the body of Jesus, Mary has turned away, and then, seeing the risen One, she has dropped on her knees and holds out her hands as if to touch him; but he, looking at her sorrowfully, gently motions her away. The whole work is simple and quaint, and very characteristic of the Beato.

The Assumption of Mary Magdalene has been frequently represented, she being borne to heaven by angels. Ribera's picture in the Louvre is a triumph of that master's composition and colour, and is a delightful example of his art since it has none of the repulsive features of many of his pictures. In too many cases the Magdalene of the Assumptions might as suitably be called a Venus or a Cleopatra, upheld by cupids.

Above the high altar in the Madeleine, at Paris, is Marochetti's marble group representing this subject. The saint is borne upward by two angels, while on each side an archangel kneels in adoration.

In considering the many artistic subjects illustrating the life of Mary Magdalene, and showing the importance of her consideration in the Church, — only a portion of which I have mentioned, — and reflecting upon the manner of their representation, I recall with sympathy Mrs. Jameson's words: " In how few instances has the result been satisfactory to mind or heart, or soul or sense! . . . A noble creature, with strong sympathies and a strong will, with powerful faculties of every kind, working for good or evil, —

such a woman Mary Magdalene must have been, even in her humiliation; and the feeble, girlish, commonplace, and even vulgar women who appear to have been usually selected as models by the artists, turned into Magdalenes by throwing up their eyes and letting down their hair, ill represent the enthusiastic convert or the majestic patroness."

The name of *St. Geneviève of Paris* is rarely heard outside of France, and her place in Art is in the French school. A peasant shepherdess, remarkable for her piety at a very early age, it was revealed — according to tradition — to the Bishop of Auxerre, when the child was but seven years old, that she was predestined to perform glorious works in the service of Christ. The bishop hung about her neck a chain on which was a coin, bearing the sign of the cross, and solemnly consecrated Geneviève to God's service.

From this moment the little maiden regarded herself as separated from the world, and many wonderful deeds are attributed to her.

But the chief example of her Heaven-sent power was given when Attila, with his Huns, besieged Paris. Then Geneviève addressed the terrified people, beseeching them not to fly before the barbarians, from whom God would surely deliver them. While she eloquently pleaded and the people hesitated, news was brought assuring them that the pagans had withdrawn from the city and marched in another direction. Then the inhabitants fell at her feet, and from that time Geneviève performed many miracles of healing and consolation, and was greatly reverenced.

When Childeric took the city of Paris he respected Geneviève; and through her influence King Clovis and Queen Clotilde were converted to Christianity, and the first Christian church in Paris was built upon Mont St. Geneviève, as the eminence was called, in her honour. Dying when eighty-nine years old, the saint was interred by the side of the sovereigns whom she had converted.

The splendid Church of St. Geneviève, now better known as the Pantheon, can scarcely be considered a suitable memorial of this humble, holy woman. The commemorative monuments of modern days are often quite out of keeping with the characters of the persons thus honoured, and Paris furnishes two notable examples of this in the churches dedicated to SS. Mary Magdalene and Geneviève.

The symbols of this peasant saint are a lighted taper, a breviary, and a demon crouching at her feet with a pair of bellows, referring to the legend that demons constantly extinguished the tapers

she burned in honour of God, which she
as constantly relighted by prayer. The
earliest representations of Geneviève show
her with all these symbols, and wearing
a veil, but later she has been pictured
as a simple shepherdess with her distaff
and spindle, and her sheep near at hand.
Occasionally she has a book, a loaf of
bread, or a basket of food, in allusion to
her charities.

The numerous pictures of St. Geneviève in the churches and galleries of
France are easily recognised, and no
special description of them is required.
They are not impressive as a rule, and
even the painting in the dome of the
Pantheon, in which the saint receives
the homage of four kings, is in question-
able taste.

It is interesting to note that more
than nine centuries after the God-inspired
bravery of St. Geneviève had saved Paris

from its enemies, another peasant maiden, *Jeanne d'Arc*, by the command of her "voices" led the army of France to victory; and now, more than four centuries and a half having elapsed since her death, this Holy Maid of France is about to be canonised.

She has already been declared "Venerable," that is, worthy of veneration, and the second title of "Blessed," and the third of Saint, will doubtless follow at no distant day. I have already seen a window, recently placed in a chapel in Georgetown, D. C., on which she is presented as an object of religious veneration.

Pictures of Jeanne d'Arc represent her as listening to the voices which directed her to raise the siege of Orleans and conduct Charles VII. to be crowned at Rheims; in her interview with Charles at Chinon, when she said: "Gentle dauphin, my name is Joan the

Maid, the King of Heaven hath sent me to your assistance; if you please to give me troops, by the grace of God and the force of arms, I will raise the siege of Orleans, and conduct you to be crowned at Rheims, in spite of your enemies;" again, when armed and riding to conquest, or on foot leading the attack at Orleans; in the scene of the coronation in the cathedral at Rheims; the Maid at her trial, and, lastly, the scene of her martyrdom.

The pictures illustrating her life, on the walls of the Pantheon, by Lenepveu, are most interesting. That in which Jeanne leads the attack on the besieging army, on foot, is spirited and full of motion. The Coronation Scene is most impressive; Jeanne, standing in the midst of the cathedral, appears as the moving spirit of this important event, as indeed she was.

The decorations for the cathedral at Domremy, by Boutet de Monvel — which are still in progress — are of the greatest possible interest, and no doubt many of those who have seen his recent exhibitions in this country will make pilgrimages to the birthplace of "the Maid," when these pictures are in their destined location. Together with the temple thus consecrated to her memory, in the midst of the scene in which she actually lived and evolved her saintly and patriotic impulses and character, they will constitute an important and fitting monument to the second peasant maiden who so gloriously saved the honour of France, and through base ingratitude lost her own life.

The story of *St. Elizabeth of Hungary* presents to us a woman who was the very ideal of Christian charity, love, and tenderness; and when we remember that most of what is related of her is historically true, — with so little of the mystical that it also appears to be true, — the interest in her is greatly enhanced.

She was the daughter of the King of Hungary, and was born in 1207. From her cradle the loveliness of her person and her character was so remarkable that its fame reached the ears of Hermann of Thuringia, who dwelt in the Castle of Wartburg. The visitors to his court brought news of the little princess, and so wonderful and charming did these reports make her to be, that Hermann sent an ambassador to ask her hand in marriage with his son Louis.

Thus it happened that Elizabeth, when but four years old, was carried to the Wartburg to be reared with the boy who was to be her husband. Here they were constant companions and playmates, even sleeping in the same cradle, and loving

each other fondly through all their child-
hood. The room which Elizabeth occu-
pied at the castle is now carefully shown
to visitors, because in it Martin Luther
lived and worked at his translation of the
Bible.

When still a mere child Elizabeth practised such works of charity as were possible. She saved the scraps of food from
the table, and sometimes ate sparingly
herself, that she might better fill her
basket to carry to the poor of Eisenach.
So long as Hermann of Thuringia lived
Elizabeth was peacefully permitted to do
as she liked, but he died when she was
nine years old, and those to whose care
she was left found her humility and Christian graces but little to their liking in the
maiden destined to preside at their court.
The aunt and sisters of Louis treated her
most unkindly, all of which she bore with
patient sorrow. Louis, however, watched

her tenderly, and when he reached his twentieth year he married her.

Elizabeth, now feeling her new responsibilities, redoubled the fervour of her piety, and even imposed severe penances on herself for her own sins and those of her people. Louis sometimes reproved her zeal, but secretly felt that he and all about her must profit by her devotions. Being told by her confessor that food for the royal table was taken from the people unjustly, and fearing lest she should eat of this, she often took but a piece of bread and a cup of water at the royal banquets.

Louis remonstrated with her, and one day drank from her cup in a playful spirit, when, to his surprise, he tasted a more delicious wine than he had ever drunk, and calling the cup-bearer he demanded the name of this vintage. But the cup-bearer declared that he had poured water only for his mistress, to which Louis made no reply, as he had already suspected that Elizabeth was cared for by angels.

Having, on an occasion when Louis made a splendid feast, given her royal mantle to a beggar who asked aid in the name of Christ, she greatly feared that Louis would upbraid her; but when she entered her chamber the mantle had been miraculously restored, and she wore it to the feast, where the guests were amazed at her beauty, for there was a light about her which was dazzling and more celestial than earthly in its glory.

Again, she so pitied a poor leprous child, who had been cast out to die, that she gathered him in her arms and put him in her own bed. Her mother-in-law, furious at this, called Louis to see what Elizabeth had done, and he found there a beautiful infant, who smiled on him and then disappeared. These are examples of the miraculous tests which Our Lord was believed to employ for the trial of the faith of his servants, and whether he assumed the form of a loathsome beggar or a leprous child, Elizabeth was true to her Christian character.

Louis feared that in her charities she exposed her health, and meeting her one day, as he was going up to the castle and she was going down, with but a single attendant, he observed that she had in her apron what seemed a heavy burden; it was, in truth, a variety of food for the poor. She was much disturbed when Louis asked what she carried, and feared his displeasure; but loosing her apron, showed him, and was herself astonished to see many red and white roses.

Then Louis would have kissed her, but so radiant was her face he dared not touch her, and, taking one of the roses, he bade her go on her way.

In 1226 Louis was in Italy, and his people were afflicted by famine and plague. Elizabeth devoted herself to the children of Eisenach, who called her, "Mother, mother," and clung to her skirts whenever she appeared. She founded a hospital for them, and, besides emptying the treasury, she sold her own jewels for charity. When Louis returned she met him with their children, saying: "See! I have given the Lord what is his, and he has preserved what is ours!" and Louis could not chide her for what she had done.

Then Louis joined the third Crusade, and died in Jerusalem. His brothers now persecuted Elizabeth, but when the knights who had gone with Louis returned with his body, they insisted that she should have justice, and the city of Marburg was given her as her dower. Thither she went with her children, and, as she already wore the cord of St. Francis, she desired to give all she possessed to the poor, and beg her way through the world. This her confessor would not permit, but she gave away all that she could, and earned money to increase her gifts by spinning. Thus taxing her strength by labour and penance, she faded from the world when but twenty-four years old.

In pictures St. Elizabeth of Hungary should be young and beautiful, and Italian artists so represented her, but some German painters made her mature, and even elderly. Her symbols are roses, red and white, such as are said to bloom in Paradise; she also has a crown, and sometimes even three are given her, to signify her blessedness as a virgin, wife, and widow; a beggar is usually seen near her.

In Fra Angelico's picture in the Academy of Perugia, the roses are seen in her apron, and she wears a crown, indicating her rank.

Holbein's picture in the Munich Gallery is very attractive. The saint is in royal attire, with a crown and aureole. Her face is serious, and her bearing dignified. On one side of her, and half-way concealed by her robe, is a kneeling beggar; on the other side, two are partly hidden in the same way, but one of them holds forward a bowl, into which the saint is pouring milk. In the background the Castle of the Wartburg is seen. This picture is most easy and natural as a whole, and the saint herself is a refined and elegant woman. Originally this work made a wing to an altar-piece executed in Augsburg, about 1516, by Hans Holbein the younger, although sometimes attributed to his father.

But all other pictures of St. Elizabeth of Hungary are overshadowed by that of

Murillo, painted for the Charity Hospital
at Seville, and now in the Academy of
San Fernando, at Madrid.   Here the
saint, in the dress of a nun, is in attend-
ance on the poor in one of the halls of
her hospital, and is engaged in washing
the scalled head of a beggar boy, from
which the work is called in Spanish *el
Tiñoso.*   Other unpleasant-looking beggars are about her in close contact with
the exquisite ladies of Elizabeth's court,
who are evidently not in sympathy with
their queen, although they aid her by
holding such articles as she requires in
her work.   Behind them is an old woman
in spectacles, peering over to see what
the saint is doing.   It has been said of
this work that the figure of the saint
equals the best pictures of Vandyck;
that the beggar-boy's face would have
done credit to Veronese, and the old
woman to Velasquez.   When one studies

this picture he is as much disgusted by its sickening exhibitions of repulsive disease as are the court ladies near the queen, but, — as Mr. Stirling remarks in his "Artists of Spain," after noticing the extreme realism and the lifelike effect of the scene, — "the high-born dame continues her self-imposed task, her pale and pensive countenance betraying no inward repugnance, and her dainty fingers shrinking from no service that can alleviate human misery and exemplify her devotion to her Master."

St. Francis of Assisi, known as the *Padre Serafico*, the founder of the Order of the Franciscans, is of great importance in the study of saints in Art. The parent convent and church of this Order, at Assisi, was, during three hundred years, the scene of the achievements of many notable artists, and remains to this day one of the most frequented, interesting, and instructive of the splendid edifices decorated by the painters and sculptors of the Renaissance.

Again, in Florence, the Church of Santa-Croce is a famous monument of this Order, in which not only excellent examples of the works of early Florentine painters, but also the wonderful sculptures of Della Robbia and Maiano, are treasured. The Church of St. Antony, in Padua, rich in frescoes, marbles and bronze; the Frari in Venice, in which Titian is buried; the Santa Maria-in-Ara-Cœli, in Rome, and many other religious institutions scattered over Italy, Spain, and other countries, are noble witnesses to the patronage of Art by the Franciscans.

Murillo owed much to these monks, who were his earliest patrons in Seville. He first painted eleven pictures for a small cloister for one of the Franciscan Mendicant Orders, and later, twenty others for the Capuchins of Seville, also Franciscans; and these were among his finest works. Indeed, could a list of the works of art executed for the churches, hospitals, and other charitable institutions of the Franciscans — in which order are the Capuchins, Minimes, Observants, Conventuals, and several others — be made, all lovers and students of Art would feel themselves their grateful debtors. Mrs. Jameson says, "Some of the grandest productions of human genius in painting, sculpture, and architecture signallised the rise of the Mendicant Orders."

The life of St. Francis is interesting from the fact that his varied personal experiences included all that would commonly be shared by several men in different walks in life. Born of a rich family, he was reared in luxury, and was famous for his love of magnificent attire and of all the so-called pleasures affected by the golden youth of all countries and periods. In the years of his prodigality he was also distinguished for his generosity, which even then foreshadowed the unselfishness of his after life.

When still but a youth, in a quarrel between Assisi and Perugia, Francis was made a prisoner, and spent a year in the fortress of Perugia, and on his release suffered a severe illness. During the months passed in prison, and on a bed of sickness, his thoughts became more serious than before, and soon after he resumed his accustomed life and rich apparel he was so moved by pity of an almost naked beggar that he gave his garments to the man, and wrapped himself in the rags of the mendicant.

At this period Francis began to have dreams, or visions, in which Christ appeared to him, and in one of these he received the command, " Francis, repair my church! it falleth in ruins!" At first he did not understand the full meaning of this charge, and incurred the anger of his father by selling goods and giving the proceeds for the reparation of the Church of St. Damiano.

At length the deeper intent of the command was revealed to him, and he abjured his former life, and dedicated himself to the service of God and to poverty. For seven years he worked in hospitals and among the poor, begging his living, and saving every penny that he could spare for the reparation of churches. He lived in a cell, went barefooted, with barely such clothes as would cover him, these being girdled with a hempen cord. Preaching Christ and his salvation, Francis made many converts, and applied to the Pope for permission to establish an Order, that he might bind his converts more closely to himself and to each other. This Innocent III. refused; but, being shown in a vision that the begging preacher merited his aid, he granted the founding of the Brotherhood, and Francis made the first condition of admission the taking of a vow of absolute poverty. In ten years from this beginning five thousand Franciscans assembled in Assisi.

Francis then went to the Orient and spent four years in austere devotion to good works. Soon after his return he had a vision which impressed on his soul that it was not by good works alone, but by divine love, that he was to become the image of Christ. When this vision had passed he found himself marked with the Stigmata, — the wounds of Jesus in his hands, feet, and side. In the eleventh canto of the " Paradise " Dante wrote:

" . . . and when
He had, through thirst of martyrdom, stood up
In the proud Soldan's presence, and there preach'd

Christ and his followers, but found the race
Unripen'd for conversion ; back once more
He hasted (not to intermit his toil),
And reap'd Ausonian lands.   On the hard rock,
'Twixt Arno and the Tiber, he from Christ
Took the last signet, which his limbs two years
Did carry.   Then the season came that He,
Who to such good had destined him, was pleased
To advance him to the meed, which he had earn'd
By his self-humbling ; to his brotherhood,
As their just heritage, he gave in charge
His dearest lady ; [1] and enjoin'd their love
And faith to her ; and, from her bosom, will'd
His goodly spirit should move forth, returning
To its appointed kingdom ; nor would have
His body laid upon another bier." [2]

The Stigmata were believed by the contemporaries of St. Francis to have been inflicted by supernatural power, and on account of these he was called the Seraphic Father, which title was also given to his Order.

[1] Poverty, whom he had wedded.
[2] He forbade any funeral pomp to be observed for him.

Two years after the death of St. Francis he was canonised, and in the same year, 1228, the foundations were laid for the church in which his relics now rest. To its erection the wealthy of all Europe contributed; Assisi supplied the marbles, and artists were sent from various parts of Italy to decorate this shrine.

The pictures of St. Francis are probably more numerous than those of any other saint. He is distinguished by his plain, cord-girdled robe, with long, loose sleeves, always of a gray colour in the oldest pictures, and changed to dark brown at about the end of the fourteenth century; a scanty cope and a hood hanging behind complete the habit. His symbols are the crucifix, the skull, the lamb, and the lily, all of which he shares with other saints, but the Stigmata are his distinguishing emblems, no other male saint having these. He has been many times represented in

ESPINOSA. — ST. FRANCIS OF ASSISI.

the act of opening his robe to disclose the wound in his side.

The most beautiful pictures of St. Francis alone represent him in a devotional attitude, with clasped hands, bending above a crucifix, looking up to one in prayer, or with uplifted eyes and ecstatic expression, apparently gazing at the glories of heaven revealed to him in visions.

Of mystical subjects, St. Francis receiving the Stigmata is very important, especially to the Franciscans. In the Upper Church at Assisi, Giotto represented this in the simplest and most childlike manner. The saint kneels in a broad landscape and raises his hands, looking to the clouds, where an angel shoots out five direct lines which apparently inflict that number of wounds on the hands, side, and feet of St. Francis. Cigoli, whose picture is in the Academy of Florence, uses nearly the same design. Other artists have elaborated it, but no picture of so mystical a subject could be other than too realistic, or even absurd. Rubens painted this ecstasy, and the picture is now in the Museum of Cologne, and is by no means a good example of his art. Agostino Caracci also represented it, and his work is in the Belvedere, Vienna, together with his picture of St. Francis in Contemplation.

A far more poetical subject, and a favourite one, is the Vision of St. Francis, in which he, a beggarly and emaciated ascetic, beholds the Virgin and child. In pictures of this subject the saint merely gazes at the glorious vision, or he holds the child in his arms, or the Virgin herself gives the child to him. The legend relates that St. Francis was in the Porzioncula when he beheld this vision; this was the small chapel, since called that of Santa Maria-degli-Angeli, at Assisi.

Almost all Spanish churches have a chapel called the Porciuncula, which is dedicated to this vision, and Murillo's picture of this subject is known by the same name. Here there are thirty-three exquisite cherubim above, who cover the saint with the beautiful red and white roses that have blossomed from the briars with which he had scourged himself. This picture is now in the Madrid Museum.

The Capuchin pictures by Murillo numbered more than twenty, seventeen of which are now in the Museum of Seville, and it has been said that the reason for the long stay of this artist in the convent — three years without once leaving it — was on account of his fear of the officers of the Inquisition, who wished to punish him for having painted the Virgin Mary with bare feet. The protection of the Capuchins, who were powerful, enabled him to pursue his art peacefully, and no works of Murillo's are more imbued with a fervent spirit of religion than are these, which were executed between 1670 and 1680.

One of these works at Seville represents another vision of St. Francis, in which the saint looks up in adoration to Christ on the cross; the Saviour has released one hand, — while the other remains nailed to the cross, — and touches the shoulder of the saint, as if in blessing; two angels hover above the scene.

A picture very frequently mentioned is St. Francis espousing Poverty, Chastity, and Obedience. Giotto painted this subject in several scenes on the walls of the Lower Church of Assisi. Interesting as they are in themselves, and as the work of Giotto, this interest is largely increased by the apparently well-founded belief that the artist received many suggestions regarding these pictures from Dante, who was a friend of Giotto.

Of Giotto's four scenes, the first represents the vow to Poverty, of which Dante wrote :

" A dame, to whom none openeth pleasure's gate
   More than to death, was, 'gainst his father's will,
   His stripling choice : and he did make her his,
   Before the spiritual court, by nuptial bonds,
   And in his father's sight : from day to day,
   Then loved her more devoutly."

In Giotto's picture a woman, Poverty, stands among thorns, and is given in marriage to the saint by Christ, while groups of angels appear as witnesses. On one side an angel conducts a youth who gives a garment to a beggar; on the other side are the rich, who are invited to approach by a second angel, but they turn away haughtily.

The allegory of Chastity is represented

by a young woman, sitting in a fortress, to whom angels pay homage. Warriors are there for the defence of the fortress; on one side St. Francis leads men forward to pay their devotions to the maiden, and on the other side, Penance, as an anchorite, drives away impurity.

The illustration of Obedience is more vague. Here, an angel in black robes places a finger of the left hand on his mouth, and with the right passes a yoke over the head of a kneeling Franciscan. St. Francis stands above this group, while two hands appear from the clouds holding the knotted cord of the Order.

In the fourth picture St. Francis, in a deacon's dress, is enthroned in glory, and surrounded by hosts of angels, who praise him with instruments and voices. These works are of remarkable interest as important among those of Giotto, who was the chief representative of this allegorical

style of painting. Kugler says: "Popes
and princes, cities and eminent monas-
teries, vied in giving him honourable
commissions, and were proud in the possession of his works."

The life of St. Francis is illustrated in
the Upper Church at Assisi in twenty-
eight pictures which have been attributed
to Giotto, but probably were executed by
different artists at various periods, as they
can be attributed to no one school or
single century.

There are many pretty stories of the
love which St. Francis showed for all
living creatures, calling them his brothers
and sisters. A picture in the series of
his life shows him preaching to birds, and
the legend gives the words which he used.
"Brother birds, greatly are ye bound to
praise the Creator, who clotheth you with
feathers, and giveth you wings to fly with,
and a purer air to breathe, and who careth

for you, who have so little care for your-
selves."

Another series of six pictures from the
life of this saint, by Ghirlandajo, is in
Santa Trinita, Florence. It is needless
to add that they are most interesting, as
are the reliefs by Maiano, in Santa Croce.
A series of small pictures by Giotto was
also painted for Santa Croce, but are now
separated, twenty being in the Academy
of Florence, four in private collections, and
two in the Berlin Gallery. Considerable
space is devoted to a discussion of these
works in Kugler's "Handbook of Painting," it having been thought that in them
a comparison is drawn between the life of
Our Lord and that of St. Francis.

An entire volume could well be devoted
to pictures of St. Francis and his disciples,
and to the serious student of Art it would
have great value. In the Gallery at Bologna is a picture of the Madonna with

SS. Paul and Francis, by Francesco Francia; in the Brera, Milan, a picture of the saint by Moretto; in the Museum of Antwerp is Rubens' picture of the Last Communion of St. Francis; in the Dresden Gallery, an Angel appearing to the Saint, by Ribera; in the Munich Pinacothek, St. Francis Healing a Paralytic, by Murillo; in the Belvedere, Vienna, SS. Francis and Andrew, by Bonifazio; in the Madrid Museum, Christ and the Virgin with St. Francis, by Murillo; in the Museum of Valencia, St. Francis and Christ on the Cross, — as already described, — by Ribalta; in the Louvre, Pope Nicholas and the Body of St. Francis, by Laurent de la Hire; in the Hermitage, St. Petersburg, the Madonna, Child, and St. Francis, by Guido Reni; and in the Academy of Florence, twelve scenes from the life of St. Francis, painted by Taddeo Gaddi after designs by Giotto.

The above are among the best works relating to this saint. Many others exist in churches and galleries, but I believe that all will be recognised from what has been written above.

St. Antony of Padua, being a Franciscan, resembles St. Francis in his habit, and among his symbols has the book and lily also; but he is distinguished by a flame of fire, which is in his hand or at his breast, by a mule kneeling, and by the infant Christ on his book or in his arms.

St. Antony, through his sympathy with persecuted Christians and martyrs, determined to become a missionary, and, through circumstances quite beyond his control, it happened that he was landed on the coast of Italy, and reached Assisi just as St. Francis held the first General Chapter of his Order, of which Antony became a member. He was a learned man, and a distinguished professor of theology in

the Universities of Bologna, Padua, and
Toulouse; but he at length resigned his
honourable position, and determined to
devote himself to teaching the common
people.

In this work his intimate knowledge of
the theological teaching of all schools, his
eloquence, his ease with all conditions of
men, and the benevolence of his manner,
conspired to render him most successful
in his self-appointed mission.

Many miracles are ascribed to St. Antony, and much of poetical and romantic
incident are mingled with the story of his
life. We are reminded of this saint by
numerous representations of him, in both
pictures and statues, but even more im-
pressively by the church which is dedicated to him in Padua.

Here his chapel, which required more
than a half century of time, and the devotion of four master sculptors and many

assistants for its completion, remains a rarely splendid monument of the marble, alabaster, bronze, gold, and silver work of the sixteenth century. Indeed, I doubt if any church in Italy is richer in monuments of great interest in the history of Art than is Sant' Antonio di Padua.

It is remarkable rather than beautiful in its exterior architecture, with six domes in an elaborate Byzantine style, rising above a Gothic basilica, and it is difficult to imagine or describe in words the effect of this arrangement.

The interior is rich in works of early Italian masters; series of bas-reliefs in bronze, the choir screen, and several other works by Donatello; frescoes by the earlier artists of the Verona school; candelabra by Andrea Riccio, which are especially fine; a few frescoes by Giotto, and some exquisite examples of goldsmith's work, and the greater part of all these devoted to the illustration of the life of Sant' Antonio.

In the *Scuolo del Santo* — school of the saint — the hall of the Brotherhood of Sant' Antonio is also rich in art treasures. Of the seventeen frescoes telling the story of the saint's life, three are by Titian, the others principally by Domenico Campagnola, a pupil of the great Venetian, who, it is said, became jealous of his disciple; at all events, the frescoes of Campagnola do not suffer by contrast with those by his master in this hall.

In the Church of San Petronio, in Bologna, there is a chapel dedicated to Sant' Antonio, in which is a statue of the saint, by Sansovino, and a series of pictures of eight miracles of St. Antony in *grisaille*, by Girolamo da Treviso. The most interesting representations of his miracles and of the prominent events in his life are, however, seen in a series of

bas-reliefs on the walls of his chapel
in Padua, which are the work of several
different sculptors.   Here, too, is the
earliest portrait of St. Antony, which
has usually been made the groundwork
of pictures of him by later artists.

Several miracles ascribed to St. Antony
are concerned with restoring life to the
dead; such pictures explain themselves,
but the so-called legend of the mule has
been many times the subject for both
painting and sculpture, and is not so easily
understood.   It is related that a heretic,
who doubted the real presence in the Sac-
rament, demanded a miracle in proof of it.
St. Antony was about to carry the Host
in procession, and meeting the mule of
the heretic on the way, the saint commanded the beast to kneel before the
consecrated wafer.   The animal obeyed
at once, and, though his master tempted
him with a portion of oats, the mule

would not rise until the Host had passed.

Vandyck painted this subject for the Recollets at Malines; it appears in almost every edifice of the Franciscan Order, and is several times repeated in Sant' Antonio di Padua, one fresco of it being by Domenico Campagnola, and a relief by Donatello.

The most attractive and beautiful pictures of St. Antony represent him with the Infant Jesus. Ludovico Caracci pictured the saint in a half-kneeling posture, holding the child lovingly in his arms, the lily being in the hands of the infant, as if he had brought it to the saint from heaven. Elisabetta Sirani's picture of St. Antony adoring the Virgin and Child is in the Bologna Gallery; in the Brera, Milan, there is a lovely Madonna and St. Antony by Vandyck; St. Antony's Vision, by Alonso Cano, is in the Pina-

cothek at Munich; a picture of SS. Paul
and Antony, by Velasquez, is in the Madrid Museum; two pictures of St. Antony
and the Infant Jesus, by Murillo, are in
the Provincial Museum of Seville, a third
is in the Hermitage, St. Petersburg, and
a fourth in the Gallery at Berlin.

The preference is given, by general
consent, to Murillo's pictures of this saint,
above those of all other artists. He
painted this subject, which seemed to fas-
cinate him, nine times, and each one of
these works is admirable, but the large
picture in the Cathedral of Seville is
doubtless the most beautiful. Of this
Stirling, in his " Artists of Spain," says:

" Kneeling near a table, the shaven
brown-frocked saint is surprised by a visit
from the Infant Jesus, a charming naked
babe, who descends in a golden flood of
glory, walking the bright air as if it were
the earth, while around him floats and

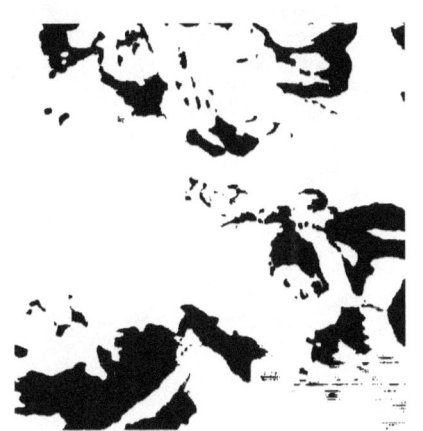

hovers a company of cherubs, most of them children, forming a rich garland of graceful forms and lovely faces. Gazing up in rapture at this dazzling vision, St. Antony kneels with arms outstretched to receive the approaching Saviour. On a table is a vase containing white lilies, the proper attribute of the saint, painted with such Zeuxis-like skill that birds wandering among the aisles — of the cathedral — have been seen attempting to perch on it and peck the flowers."

The story is current in Seville that the Duke of Wellington vainly offered the canons of the cathedral a sum of about two hundred and forty thousand dollars for this picture, and when, in 1874, the canvas was cut from its frame and stolen, all Seville was in mourning. For a long time no trace of it could be found, when two men took it to Mr. Schaus, the picture dealer in New York, and offered it to him for two hundred and fifty dollars! He recognised the work, bought it, and through the Spanish consul returned it to Seville. I have since seen it in its place, and had I not known of its wanderings I could not have imagined that the rapturous saint kneeling in the solemn cathedral had ever been thus wantonly disturbed.

I have said that St. Francis of Assisi is the only male saint to whom the *Stigmata* is given in works of art, which is, of course, equivalent to saying that no other had the supreme honour of bearing the wounds of Christ. Among female saints this is equally true of *St. Catherine of Siena*, although these marks are given to St. Maria Maddalena di' Pazzi, without authority from the saintly legends.

St. Catherine is one of the patron saints of Siena, her birthplace, and from the artists of the Sienese school she received

loyal and generous recognition. Her
father was a wealthy dyer of Siena, who
was blessed with a numerous family, of
which Catherine was the youngest. From
her infancy, — as we read of many chosen
servants of God, — she was a serious child,
who loved solitude, and seemed to be
gazing into a visionary world rather than
watching the life about her. She had
heard the story of St. Catherine of Alexandria, and when but eight years old she
dedicated herself to a religious life and
to chastity.

When older, she refused to marry, and
her parents could not forgive her pecu-
liarities, and imposed the most menial
tasks on her, hoping that hardships would
induce her to do what their wishes and
commands had failed to recommend to her.
She, however, accepted her burdens without a murmur, and laboured incessantly.
One day her father suddenly entered her

room and saw her kneeling in prayer,
while a white dove sat on her head, of
which Catherine seemed to be unconscious. This greatly affected the stub-
born dyer and convinced him that his
child was protected by the Holy Ghost.
He withdrew his opposition to her wishes,
and Catherine soon took her vows as a
penitent.

She never became a professed nun, but
she lived a most rigorous life, which was
full of spiritual temptations and a constant
struggle for peace. At length, in the
convent church, she had glorious visions,
when Jesus, her mystical spouse, appeared
to her and comforted her with sweet
counsel and his visible presence.

To the care of the most unpleasant
diseases and to all possible penances
Catherine devoted herself, and shrank
from no mortification or labour that could
benefit others. At length, in Pisa, as she

prayed before an especially sacred crucifix, she was lost in an ecstasy in which she received the Stigmata; this must have assured her of her acceptance with Christ, and brought peace to her troubled soul.

The influence which Catherine exerted in inducing the Pope, who was then at Avignon, to return to Rome, with all the diplomatic service which this required of her, is a matter of history, and is recorded in the accounts of her life. Such a record of great interest is that by Adolphus Trollope in his charming book, " A Decade of Italian Women."

Catherine of Siena died when but thirty-three years old, in 1380, full of the faith in which she had lived.

A fresco in the Church of San Domenico, in Siena, is probably the oldest picture of St. Catherine, and may be considered an actual portrait, since it was painted by Andrea Vanni, who was long a valued friend of the saint. She is represented standing, with her black mantle drawn about her; in one hand she holds a stalk of lilies, while she presents the other — on which the sacred wound is plainly seen — to a kneeling nun, who, with hands folded on her breast, reverently touches her lips to the fingers of the saint. This picture can be seen but imperfectly as it is covered with glass for its preservation.

Besides the Stigmata and the lily, the symbols of St. Catherine of Siena are the palm, a church, and a crown of thorns, as her legend relates that Christ appeared and offered her two crowns, one of gold, and a second of thorns, which last she accepted and pressed on her head until the thorns penetrated her brain.

One of the most beautiful and famous pictures of St. Catherine is known as the Madonna of the Rosary, and is in the Church of St. Sabina, in Rome. It is

by Sassoferrato, and represents SS. Dominic and Catherine kneeling before an
enthroned Madonna, who, turning to St.
Dominic, drops a rosary into his hand,
while the child gives a second rosary to
St. Catherine and presses a crown of
thorns upon her head, which is covered
by her hood. Above are two angels and
three cherub heads. The picture is well
composed, well balanced, and both dignified and elegant in effect.

In the chapel in the Church of San
Domenico, Siena, is the fresco by Razzi,
which represents St. Catherine receiving
the Stigmata. She is swooning, and supported by two nuns of her Order. The
black mantle has fallen entirely off St.
Catherine and partly off the nun who
kneels beside her; the sister who stands
behind, and bends tenderly over the saint
while still guarding her from falling, retains the black garment. By this arrange-

ment the light and shade in the work are good ; the faces of the nuns are beautiful, and the contrast between the fainting saint and the expression of reverent sympathy on the countenances of the others is very fine and most effective.

The picture of the same subject in the Borghese Gallery, Rome, shows the fainting saint supported by two angels. It is by Agostino Caracci. In one hand St. Catherine holds a lily, and with the other presses a heart to her bosom, in reference to the legend that on one occasion, when she was praying to Jesus for a new heart, he appeared, and, taking his heart from his breast, gave it to her. Here, too, the saint wears her hood, upon which rests the crown of thorns. The heads and faces of the angels are lovely, and the expression of the one who looks in the face of the saint is remarkable for its intense interest in what is occurring.

AGOSTINO CARACCI. — ST. CATHERINE OF SIENA.

Other interesting works illustrating the life of Catherine are in San Domenico, and in her oratory, once the shop of her father, which Trollope says the veneration of the Sienese has not permitted to remain as when she lived in it. The walls are covered with frescoes by Salimbeni and Pachierotti, and the altar-piece is by Sodoma.

In tracing the stories of the saints and their association with Art, from its infancy to its prime,—even in outline,—how many kinds of interest are awakened: the religious, artistic, æsthetic, romantic, poetic, and historical are all involved. The suggestiveness of such an outline to travellers or stay-at-homes is of value, and I trust that the many pleasant hours that I have spent, from time to time, during thirty-five years in searching for the history and traditions of the saints, and studying their relation to the Arts, may have gained for me the privilege of interesting others in this rich and inexhaustible subject. And I trust that in this book

"Th' unlearned their wants may view,
The learned reflect on what before they knew."

APPENDIX

APPENDIX.

AN EXPLANATION OF THE SYMBOLISM
PROPER TO REPRESENTATIONS OF THE
SAINTS.

THE circle about the heads of sacred persons is known as *the Aureole*, *the Glory*, and *the Nimbus*. Before the Christian era, such symbols, as seen on ancient coins, medals, and other objects, signified that dignity and power belonged to the person thus honoured, as to the gods. In the early centuries after Christ, even Satan was represented with a glory, as a symbol of his power, and by reason of its pagan origin this emblem was not readily adopted in Christian art; after the fifth or sixth century, however, it came into more general use, and invariably indicated divine glory, a consecrated being, and saintly blessedness.

The aureole is varied in size and form. It is a simple circle, of more or less brilliancy, about the head of representations of saints no longer living; if the saint is portrayed as still alive, the form is square; if pictured as ascending to heaven, an oblong glory surrounds the entire person, and is known as *mandorla*, or almond shaped, in Italian.

Didron, in his " Iconographie Chretienne," devotes many pages to the discussion of the various forms of glories which are seen, and designates the classes of beings for whom each one should be used, and gives the reasons by which these uses are properly governed; but the artists were not so learned as he in these distinctions, and the general idea that is given above serves ordinarily to explain the works of art with which we are familiar.

In the early centuries of our era, statues erected in the open air had metal discs fastened to the heads, as a protection from the weather, and many aureoles in ancient pictures resemble these, having the effect of metal plates behind the head.

After the twelfth century a simple golden band behind the head was much used; again, several circles are seen, and these are sometimes set with precious stones, or inscribed with the name of the saint represented. After the fifteenth century a bright circle over the head was chiefly used, until the seventeenth century, when all these glories were essentially abandoned. In more modern pictures we sometimes see this symbol, though it is not used with the careful distinctions observed by the old painters.

In pictures this emblem is always
golden; on glass and ivory it is in various colours. Didron suggests that the
colours are symbolical, as, for example,
the black nimbus on the head of Judas.
He speaks as follows of a miniature dated
1120, which represents Christ with a
nimbus and crown of gold, surrounded
by the nine orders of saints who form
the celestial court, intermingled with
angels.

"Virgins, apostles, martyrs, confessors,
prophets, patriarchs, the chaste, the
married, and lastly the penitents. The
first four orders, the most exalted of all,
have the nimbus of gold. Prophets and
patriarchs, the saints of the Old Testament, and who knew the truth imperfectly only, through the veil of metaphor
and allegory, have a nimbus of silver.
The nimbus of the chaste is red; that
of the married, green; and that of the

penitents, yellow, but slightly tinted. Colour is evidently employed in these instances as a hierarchical medium; it loses its brilliancy in proportion as it descends from a lofty to an inferior grade, after which point the title of saint is no longer awarded, and the persons represented are regarded only as ordinary mortals."

Interesting as this explanation of colour is, it must not be too seriously considered, as it is by no means true that all artists gave strict attention to the colour of aureoles. As time wore on, the only colour significance seems to me to be that yellow is the colour of gold or preciousness, while red is that of fire, and typifies zeal and passion; blue and purple being emblems of penitence.

The nimbus is, in its essential significance, a representation of light, issuing from the head, and it is not unusual to see rays surrounding the head, more especially in pictures of the persons of the Trinity. These rays are variously arranged; at times they are at regular distances, and form a circle or some other regular form on the outer line; again, three rays proceed from the top of the head, and three others from each side, and a line of light connects them, either on the outer line of the rays, or again at a distance within that line, leaving the ends of the rays beyond the circle.

The general idea that these symbols indicate sacred or holy personages, and symbolise light radiating from these beings, will give an understanding of them in all cases, although one who cares to study this point will find a world of mysticism in their comprehensive interpretation.

The Cross, when the symbol of a saint, is usually in the form of the Cross of the

Cotignola. — St. Bernard Giving the Rule of
His Order.

Crucifixion, or the Latin Cross; but St.
Andrew has the transverse or X cross,
the form on which he suffered death.
The Egyptian cross is given to St. Anthony as a symbol of his crutch, the cross-
arms making the top, and is known by
his name; the same cross is seen with the
Apostle Philip. The Greek cross is that
in which the arms are of equal length. In
some pictures of the Popes, a staff with
a double cross on top is seen, which is
never given to any ecclesiastic below the
Pope; a staff with a single cross indicates
a Greek bishop, as a crosier is the symbol
of a Latin bishop.

The Fish is a very ancient and universal
symbol of water and baptism, and was
frequently seen on ancient baptismal fonts,
and in the decoration of baptisteries. The
letters of the Greek word for fish, ΙΧΘΥΣ
form the anagram of the name of Jesus
Christ, — they give in the Latin, *Jesus*

Christus, Dei filius, Salvator, and in English, Jesus Christ, the Son of God, the Saviour. For this reason the fish became a singularly sacred symbol.

The special fish used as a pagan symbol was the dolphin, and this is seen on ancient sarcophagi, tombs of martyrs, utensils of various kinds, and as an ornament in architecture. The fish is a symbol of those saints who made many converts to Christianity, referring to the promise of Jesus, " And I will make you fishers of men." When given to St. Peter it recalls his former occupation, his conversion, and his success in making converts.

The Lion, when seen with St. Jerome and the hermit saints, is an emblem of solitude; with the martyrs it denotes death in the amphitheatre, and, when placed at the feet, is significant of exceptional courage and resolution in the face of persecution.

The Lamb is a symbol of unblemished sacrifice, of modesty, and of innocence. In the first sense it is given to St. John Baptist, and in the second to St. Agnes. In the first five centuries of the Christian era, Christ was customarily represented as a lamb, until, in 692, the Church, fearing that allegory was displacing reality and history, decreed in council that the human face and form of Christ should be substituted in works of art for the symbolic Lamb of God. It was not, however, until much later than the time of this council that Christ was generally represented in the form of a man, and was more frequently seen as the Good Shepherd who cared for the sheep.

The Peacock, which is ordinarily considered a symbol of pride, was, in ancient days, an emblem of the apotheosis — or the passing of the soul — of an empress; and as a Christian symbol it typifies the

passing of the spirit from mortal to immortal life.

The Dove is the emblem of the Holy
Ghost, and also of the soul of man; it
is seen issuing from the lips of dying
martyrs, as a symbol of the flight of the
soul to heaven. When represented as
an attribute of female saints it denotes
purity; and it is also seen beside saints
who were esteemed as especially inspired, as were some of the Fathers of
the Church.

The Crown may be the symbol of a
glorious martyrdom, or the attribute of
a royal saint, or in the case of a royal
martyr it would unite the two intentions.
This symbol is also used in a mystic
sense, to denote the "bride of Christ,"
as when it is placed on the head of a nun
at the moment of her consecration, and
doubtless had this significance also, when
indicating the glorious martyrdom of such

saints as Catherine, Lucia, and others. When on the head of the Madonna it symbolises her sovereignty as Queen of Heaven, and refers to the rank of royal saints who wear a crown or have one placed at their feet.

The Palm, as in Revelation 7:9–14, indicates a glorious martyrdom. It is represented in a great variety of ways, and angels frequently descend from heaven to confer it on those who have suffered for the sake of their Christian faith. With the ancients, the palm denoted victory over the enemy, and to the Christian it is emblematic of the spiritual victory over sin and death.

The Sword, when given to warrior saints, is an attribute, but like the *axe*, *lance*, and *club*, the sword is frequently the symbol of a violent death.

Arrows, signifying the manner of their martyrdom, are given to SS. Ursula,

Christina, and Sebastian. In the same sense *wheels* are represented with St. Catherine; the *poniard* with St. Lucia; *pincers* and *shears* with SS. Apollonia and Agatha; and the *cauldron* with SS. John the Evangelist and Cecilia.

The Skull is a symbol of penance, and the *shell* of pilgrimage.

The Bell is given to St. Anthony as a means of exorcising evil spirits or demons.

Fire and *Flames* symbolise religious fervour, punishment, and martyrdom.

The Flaming Heart is emblematic of fervent piety, and is a symbol of several saints, both men and women.

The Anchor symbolises patience and hope, and is seen on very ancient objects, such as antique gems. It was much used in the symbolic decoration of the Catacombs.

The Banner is an emblem of victory,

and is given to military saints and victo-
rious martyrs. SS. Ursula and Reparata
are the female saints to whom it belongs.

The Church is a symbol of a founder
of a church, but when represented with
St. Jerome it is an emblem of the whole
Catholic Church. When rays of light
issue from the portal, they are emblematic of the light which emanates from
the Christian Church.

The Olive, the symbol of peace, is given
to SS. Agnes and Pantaleon. It is much
used in the decoration of tombs and fune-
real monuments.

The Lily is a symbol of purity, and is
given to SS. Catherine of Siena, Francis
of Assisi, Anthony of Padua, Dominic
and others.

The Unicorn is a very ancient symbol
of purity. It is represented with St. Justina only.

The Book is an emblem of the Gospel,

of the learning of certain saints, and of authorship.

The Lamp, Taper, or Lantern symbolise wisdom and piety; in the hand of St. Lucia such an emblem is significant of her celestial wisdom.

The Chalice is an emblem of faith, and is given to SS. Barbara and John. When the serpent is in the cup it is a symbol of wisdom.

The Scourge symbolises penance, and usually indicates that which is self-inflicted by the saint to whom it is given. In rare cases, as in that of St. Ambrose, it refers to the penance prescribed for others.

The Ship is an emblem of the Church. It is, however, associated with the legends of certain saints, as SS. Ursula, Nicholas, and Peter.

Fruit and *Flowers* are lovely symbols; roses are associated with the exquisite legends of SS. Cecilia, Dorothea, and .

Elizabeth of Hungary. An apple, pear, or pomegranate belong to St. Catherine, as the mystical bride of Christ. In the Old Testament the apple was significant of the fall of man; in the New Testament it is an emblem of the redemption from that fall, and as such is represented in pictures of the Madonna and Infant Jesus.

The Crucifix, when held in the hand, is the attribute of a preacher; it is also a symbol of devout faith, and has a special significance in pictures of St. Catherine of Siena, who received the Stigmata.

The Standard with the *Cross* is seen in pictures of missionaries and preachers, when it is emblematic of the triumph of Christianity; it is also seen with warrior saints and those of royal blood who belonged to the Monastic Orders.

The Crown of Thorns is seen on the head of St. Catherine of Siena, and is also occasionally represented with other saints, signifying suffering for Christ's sake.

A Sun is sometimes represented on the breast of St. Thomas Aquinas, and occasionally in pictures of other saints; it is symbolic of the light of Wisdom.

Beggars, Children, Lepers, and Slaves, with broken chains, when at the feet of a saint are symbolic of charity; they are frequently of diminutive size.

Several of the above symbols — the lily, rose, olive, apple, pomegranate, book, and dove — are seen in pictures of the Madonna, as well as in those of the saints, and have the same significance in all cases; the double use of these symbols can cause no confusion, as the Madonna pictures are unmistakable. The serpent, however, has two meanings; in the chalice of St. John the Evangelist it symbolises wisdom; in pictures of the Madonna it is an emblem of sin, or of Satan, and is gen-

FRA BARTOLOMMEO — ST. BRIDGET OF SWEDEN
GIVING THE RULE TO HER NUNS.

erally beneath her feet, in reference to the text, "And I will put enmity between thee and the woman, and between thy seed and her seed; it shall bruise thy head."

The Hart is an emblem of solitude, purity, and spiritual aspiration. "Like as the hart panteth after the water-brooks, so panteth my soul for thee, O God." With St. Hubert or St. Eustace it is a symbol of the miraculous stag which appeared to them; or again, of the hind that spoke to St. Julian, or the doe in the legend of St. Giles.

The Dragon, the emblem of sin and Satan, the spiritual foe of mankind, is represented with SS. Michael and Margaret, to symbolise their conquest of evil; with SS. Sylvester and George it is an emblem of the paganism which they overcame; with St. Martha it is a symbol of a devouring flood, such as the inundation of the Rhone in her lifetime.

In early religious art colours were used with special significance, and great care was taken to give them their appropriate place and to deepen the symbolism of pictures by their proper arrangement.

White was emblematic of chastity in a woman, of integrity and humility in a man.

Red, in a good sense, symbolised love, the Holy Spirit, royalty, and heat. White and red roses were emblems of love, innocence, and wisdom. In a bad sense, red was a symbol of hatred, war, blood, and punishment. Red and black combined symbolised purgatory and the devil.

Green was an emblem of spring, hope, and victory, while *Blue* symbolised heaven, truth, fidelity, the firmament, and penitence.

Yellow, in a good sense, was the emblem of the sun, beneficence, marriage, fruitfulness, and faith; thus St. Joseph and St. Peter are clothed in yellow. In its bad sense it indicates jealousy and deceit. Judas was represented in a dingy yellow, with few exceptions, when a dirty brown was used; but so rarely was the ugly yellow omitted from pictures of the traitor, it came to be called " Judas colour."

Gray was symbolic of mourning and of innocence unjustly accused. *Violet* was emblematic of passion and suffering, or of love, truth, and penitence.

As each Order of monks wore a habit of a special colour it is not difficult to distinguish them in pictures, and by this means one can usually know for what Order the work in question was painted.

The *Benedictines* wore black originally, and for that reason were called *Monaci Neri*, — Black Monks, — but the Reformed Benedictines adopted the white habit, and St. Benedict himself is represented in both colours, according to the Order for which the picture was painted.

The *Franciscans* originally wore gray, but the Reformed Communities of that Order adopted the dark brown habit. The hempen cord as a girdle is, however, an unfailing characteristic of the Franciscan monk. The black habit presents some difficulties, as it is worn by the *Augustines*, the *Servi*, the *Oratorians*, and the *Jesuits*.

The same perplexity occurs in the case of a white habit, as it is worn by *Cistercians* and several other Orders, among which are the *Trappists*, *Camaldolesi*, and *Trinitarians*.

The *Dominicans* wear black over white, and the *Carmelites* and *Premonstratensians* reverse these colours, wearing white over black.

The illustration which shows St. Bernard giving Rules to his Order, the Cistercians, well displays the white habit of these monks, over which the founder wears a rich vestment, and also a mitre, as Abbot of Clairvaux. Several religious symbols are also introduced here. This picture is in the Berlin Gallery.

The picture of St. Bridget of Sweden giving the Rule to her Nuns, is of the same character; it is in Santa Maria Nuova Florence.

The Abbess of the Brigittines wears a black habit and cloak, white wimple, and white veil, while the nuns have a gray habit and black hood, with a red band around the head, and across the top, to distinguish the habit from that of the Benedictine orders.

It requires but little study to familiarise one with the symbols and other distinguishing characteristics of religious pictures, while a knowledge of them explains much that is not comprehended without it, and greatly enhances the enjoyment of these works.

THE END.

INDEX.